JAN 1 2 2008

Messenger of Love

Also by Barbara Cartland in Large Print:

Love in the Ruins
The Love Pirate
The Love Puzzle
The Loveless Marriage
Lovers in Lisbon
Lucky Logan Finds Love
A Night of Gaiety
No Time for Love
Ola and the Sea Wolf
Passage to Love
The Prude and the Prodigal
The Queen of Hearts
Secret Harbor

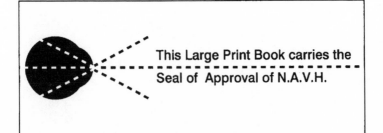

Messenger of Love

Barbara Cartland

Thorndike Press • Waterville, Maine

Published in 2005 by arrangement with Cartland Promotions.

Thorndike Press® Large Print Candlelight.

The tree indicium is a trademark of Thorndike Press.

The text of this Large Print edition is unabridged.
Other aspects of the book may vary from the original edition.

Set in 16 pt. Plantin by Al Chase.

Printed in the United States on permanent paper.

Library of Congress Cataloging-in-Publication Data

Cartland, Barbara, 1902–
    Messenger of love / by Barbara Cartland.
       p. cm. — (Thorndike Press large print candlelight)
    ISBN 0-7862-8028-X (lg. print : hc : alk. paper)
    1. Great Britain — History — Elizabeth, 1558–1603 —
Fiction. 2. Elizabeth I, Queen of England, 1533–1603 —
Fiction. 3. Courts and courtiers — Fiction. 4. Large type
books. I. Title. II. Thorndike Press large print Candlelight
series.
PR6005.A765M47 2005
823′.912—dc22   2005017838

Messenger of Love

As the Founder/CEO of NAVH, the only national health agency solely devoted to those who, although not totally blind, have an eye disease which could lead to serious visual impairment, I am pleased to recognize Thorndike Press★ as one of the leading publishers in the large print field.

Founded in 1954 in San Francisco to prepare large print textbooks for partially seeing children, NAVH became the pioneer and standard setting agency in the preparation of large type.

Today, those publishers who meet our standards carry the prestigious "Seal of Approval" indicating high quality large print. We are delighted that Thorndike Press is one of the publishers whose titles meet these standards. We are also pleased to recognize the significant contribution Thorndike Press is making in this important and growing field.

Lorraine H. Marchi, L.H.D.
Founder/CEO
NAVH

★ Thorndike Press encompasses the following imprints: Thorndike, Wheeler, Walker and Large Print Press.

1

The coach turned slowly into the courtyard of the Palace of Greenwich. It was old fashioned, cumbersome and thickly splashed with mud and dust as if it had travelled a long way. The horses drawing it were obviously tired and the coachman guiding them seemed to hesitate and check the leaders as if uncertain of his directions.

A group of gallants walking in the sunshine drew aside to let the coach pass. As they did so, there was a sudden sharp sound, the hind wheel slowly left the axle and with a crack and a groan the coach subsided on the cobbles.

It was so unexpected that for a moment the group of gentlemen, in their colourful doublets and plumed hats could only gasp at the spectacle. And then one of them exclaimed:

'By God! The Ark has arrived in London and finds itself at a loss on dry land!'

His laughter, robust and untrammelled, rang out just as the face of a girl appeared at the window of the coach sprawled untidily on the cobbles. She stared at the speaker with his head thrown back and shaking sides, and at the gallants surrounding him with their wide mouths before she said curtly:

'Is there a gentleman amongst you who has the courtesy to assist me?'

Her voice silenced the laughter and the gallant who had laughed first moved forward to wrench open the door.

'I thank you, Sir,' she said, and there was irony in her tone. 'And would it be too much to ask one of your friends to help with the horses? My coachman is old and may find it difficult to hold them.'

The horses were, in fact, too tired to cause much trouble. They had plunged for a moment when the coach had suddenly become a dead weight behind them, but now the coachman had them well under control.

After a quick glance the man to whom she had spoken replied:

'The animals are giving no trouble, Madam.'

She laid her fingers in his. It was a small hand, soft and warm, for she had removed her gloves, and he was suddenly conscious that the eyes that she raised to his were vividly blue against the pink and white of a complexion which could only have come from the country.

'May I lift you, Madam?' he enquired. 'You will find it hard to reach the ground without a step.'

'Thank you, but I am not decrepit,' she answered and, holding on to his hand, sprang on to the ground with a lightness that was almost indescribable.

He saw then how small she was, her head barely coming to his shoulder; and he was also aware, somewhat vaguely, that her gown was out of date and her ruff of a pattern that had been worn five years earlier.

On the other hand, she realised that the man looking down at her was dressed in the very height of fashion. His doublet was slashed with crimson velvet, his small ruff was piped with gold and he carried a pair of gloves embroidered with the same roses which decorated his shoes.

He was not more resplendent than his friends, although there was about him an air of authority combined with what seemed to her an arrogance which was insupportable. It was apparent in the manner in which his velvet hat was placed over one eye and in the way he stood looking down at her with his grey eyes twinkling and a smile of cynical amusement at the corners of his mouth.

She felt the anger which had smouldered at his mockery burst into flame.

'I thank you, Sir, for your assistance,' she said haughtily. 'And now I have no further need either of your services or of your laughter.'

There was a sudden silence after she had spoken and she felt her heart give a quick, frightened thump because she had been rude and because it was not in her nature to attack any one. But somehow he had infuriated her, not only by what he had said but by the very manner in which he had stood there, it seemed to her, relishing her discomfiture.

She heard one of his friends snigger and say something behind his hand; but the man whom she had attacked appeared quite unabashed. He lifted his feather hat with a grandiose gesture and swept it before him until its feathers touched the ground.

'I am at your service, Madam, whenever you should require me.'

She turned away from him petulantly and spoke to the coachman.

'I will send you help from the stables,' she said.

'Thank ye, Mistress Andora,' the coachman replied. 'The poor beasties will give no trouble. They be ready to sleep where they be a-standing.'

'We have driven them hard,' Andora said. 'And we must be grateful that the coach got us here before it collapsed. You will be able to have it mended, Barker?'

'Oi 'opes so,' he answered. 'Oi 'opes so, indeed.'

'May I not send some of my own coach-builders to the rescue?' a voice asked.

Andora turned to see that he was still beside her. Still with that hateful smile on his face and the amusement in his eyes. The words rose hotly to her lips to refuse him and then she remembered that she knew no one in this vast place. She did not even know which was the right door for her to enter.

As if he understood her hesitation and the thoughts that were running through her head, he said:

'Perhaps I should introduce myself. I am Hengist Wake, at your service. And you?'

'I am Andora Bland,' she replied. 'I have come to London to be in attendance upon Her Majesty.'

'Another Maid of Honour!' he exclaimed. 'Their numbers grow day by day — and each more lovely than the last. What a galaxy of beauty to bemuse and bewilder a mere man!'

Andora turned her head away from him as if she was not interested in his conversation but wished to get on with the business of having her coach moved and the horses taken to their stalls.

She heard a quick order and then, as if by magic it seemed, servants appeared, the horses were taken from the shafts, the old coachman was helped down from the box and her trunks and valuables were carried ahead of her. Now only the coach itself remained, sprawling a little drunkenly in the sunshine.

'Now, Mistress Bland, may I escort you?'

She pulled herself up with a little effort of pride, conscious suddenly that she, too, was tired and that the journey had been long and tedious.

'I would not trespass any further on your kindness, Sir,' she answered.

He smiled at her as if she was being fractious and obstinate; a child who had to be driven into doing what was required of her.

'Come,' he said peremptorily. 'The door you want is to the left of where we are standing. If you go through the main entrance, you will find it much farther to the Queen's apartments.'

Obediently, because there seemed no other course left for her to take, Andora

walked beside him across the sunlit courtyard. She was thankful that his friends did
not accompany them; but she heard a laugh
behind her and guessed there was something about her that amused them, even as
her companion had been amused at her
coach.

Quite suddenly she felt panic-stricken.
Why had she come here? Why had she left
the country and the home that she loved to
come to this place where she would seem
gauche and out of place?

She had a sudden longing for the red brick
house overlooking the quiet parkland, with
the deer resting in the shadows under the
trees. Why, why had she been such a fool as
to agree to leave everything she loved
behind?

'You have come a long distance?'

The question broke in on her thoughts.

'Yes, a long way,' she answered, determined to tell him nothing.

'Your name is Bland. Any relation to Sir
Robert Bland?'

'He is my father.'

'Indeed! Then I am honoured to meet his
daughter. Everyone knows how devotedly
and with what courage your father fought
for Her Majesty.'

'I will tell my father, when I write, of the

13

kind things you have said about him,' Andora said a little stiffly.

'And so another Bland comes to Court!' the voice beside her remarked. Somehow she fancied there was a note of derision in it because she was so small and insignificant in comparison with her father and his deeds of valour.

A man approaching them stopped.

'Sir Hengist,' he said. 'My Lord Essex is asking for you.'

'Tell my Lord that I will be with him very shortly,' Sir Hengist replied.

Andora glanced at him under her eyelashes. So he was a knight, she thought, obviously one of the important people of the Court. But that did not make her like him any better. She could still hear the scorn in his voice when he had referred to her coach as the Ark. She could see, even without looking at him, the amusement which still curled the corners of his lips.

'I would not detain you if you have other business, Sir,' she said hastily.

'Can there be any business more important than escorting a lovely woman?' he asked.

Again she felt that he was mocking her. It was quite a distance to the door he had indicated and every step made her realise how

14

strange she must look compared with the resplendent creature who walked beside her.

There were other women in the courtyard and she saw only too well how badly her gown compared with theirs. She had been so proud of her clothes before she had left home. They had been specially made for her by the whole household, who had sat up late night after night stitching lace on silk and velvet and embroidering little motifs on bodices which she now saw, with a sense of despair, were cut in entirely the wrong shape.

She was not so stupid as not to acknowledge to herself, after only a glance at the elegant ladies lifting their voluminous skirts over the cobbles, that almost everything she had brought with her was countrified and out-of-date. Again she longed to run away, to go home, and knew with a sense almost of despair that anyway it was impossible until her coach was mended.

'Here is the door,' she heard Sir Hengist say. 'And if you take the staircase on the right and follow the Long Gallery to the far end, you will find the entrance to the Queen's apartments.'

'I thank you.'

Andora wondered whether she should hold out her hand to him or whether it was enough to drop him a curtsy. She did the latter and again he swept her that extravagant bow.

'I hope you will be very happy here, Mistress Andora,' he said.

'I hope so too,' she said in a low voice. 'B . . . but I doubt it.'

'Why?' he asked curiously.

She answered him though she felt she should not linger.

'I am used to the country. I do not understand Court ways or Court people.'

'You must not judge them all by me,' Sir Hengist said, and she heard the laughter in his voice.

Pride drove back the tears and made her lift up her chin, suddenly angry with him again.

'Do you always laugh at the misfortunes of other people?' she enquired.

'Invariably,' he replied, 'and at my own as well.'

He bowed to her again and then turned and left her staring after him, not certain whether she was sorry to see him go because it left her entirely alone, or glad because she disliked him.

Slowly she went up the stairs trying to remember that she was her father's daughter — Mistress Andora Bland of Willow Park.

That meant something in the County of Hertfordshire, but here she was certain no one had heard of it. But at least they had heard of her father. Even Sir Hengist Wake had spoken of him with a touch of reverence in his voice; for that, at least, she ought to forgive him for his laughter and his mockery.

She walked slowly along the Gallery. Through the windows she could see the river, flowing silver beyond green lawns. In it there were the sails of many fine ships. She would have liked to stop and watch them, but she felt this was not the time to day-dream.

She had been summoned imperiously to come to Court. *Send your daughter with all possible despatch,* the Queen had written to her father. She had imagined that because of the tone of the letter the Queen had been in need of further Maids of Honour. But now Sir Hengist had said they were arriving day after day. Why and wherefore such haste?

Her father had been delighted at the summons.

'So I am not forgotten after all,' he had said. 'I had imagined when my health drove me from giving further service to our Queen that she might have forgotten me. But she

17

never forgets. She remembers everything. A woman without peer in the whole history of England. Remember that, Andora. There has never been a woman like her.'

'Yes, Father, I will remember,' Andora had said. Sometimes she felt impatient, or perhaps it was jealous, of the admiration that her father expended so unstintingly on the Queen.

'Why does Father talk so much about the Queen, Mother?' she had asked when she was only a child.

'Your father fought for and served our Queen until his health would permit him to do no more,' her mother answered. 'We are all Her Majesty's loyal subjects, Andora.'

'Yes, yes, of course,' Andora said. 'But Father talks of her so much. He makes her . . . Well, he makes her out to be . . . hardly human.'

'Perhaps she is not,' her mother said with a smile, and then she put her arms round Andora and kissed her.

'Do not worry your head about such matters,' she had said. 'Go and play in the garden. If it amuses your father to talk of the old days, what does it matter to us? He is a fighting man, a man who likes to be in the thick of everything, a man who is used to roaring with the lions of England. He finds us little country mice somewhat boring, I fear.'

'Little country mice!' Andora could hear her mother's voice saying the words now and she thought, with a little rueful smile, that is exactly what she was — a little country mouse come to town!

Almost reluctantly her hand went up to knock on the door at the very end of the Gallery. Mice should stay in their own homes, she thought, and not put their heads into the lion's den.

The door was opened by a porter. He noted her name without interest; and when she said she was a new Maid of Honour to Her Majesty, he took her down the passage to Mistress Blanche Parry, the Chief Gentlewoman of the Privy Chamber.

Mistress Parry, who was seated in the sitting-room of her own apartment, was old and she had grown grey in the service of the Queen. She smiled kindly as Andora curtsied before her.

'I am relieved to see you, child,' she said. 'We have had reports that the roads were water-logged with the recent rains and were half afraid that you would find it impossible to reach us so quickly.'

'Some of the fords were very high, Madam,' Andora said, 'but my coach managed to cross them. It was only when I actually arrived here at Greenwich that it lost a wheel.'

'How terrible for you!' Mistress Parry said, clasping her hands together. 'Had it happened earlier, you might have been forced to wait hours by the roadside.'

'No, indeed, Madam, I should have ridden one of the horses. It might have been an unconventional way to arrive, but at least I should have got here,' Andora said.

Mistress Parry smiled.

'I see you are a young woman of resource,' she said. 'Has your luggage and, indeed, your damaged coach been attended to?'

'A gentleman who saw the accident promised me his help,' Andora said.

'Did you learn his name?'

'Yes, Sir Hengist Wake.'

She saw the look of surprise on Mistress Parry's face, and she saw an expression of something else which she could not quite place before the lady said:

'Then rest assured everything will be done. Sir Hengist is a person of some importance.'

There was a reserved note in her tone which told Andora that she did not approve of Sir Hengist.

'And now I will take you to the Queen,' Mistress Parry said. 'She asked to be informed of your arrival.'

She led the way from the room and down long, twisting passages. Andora longed for time to wash her hands and to tidy herself before being ushered into the Royal presence, but she was too shy to suggest it and merely wondered why Her Majesty required to see her so speedily.

Mistress Parry opened the door into a small room. It was obviously an antechamber and there was no one in it save a maid, who curtsied and withdrew. There was a door into another room and Mistress Parry went towards it. As she did so, it opened and a loud voice was heard saying:

'God's teeth! Am I to wait interminably for despatches that should have been here this past hour or more? Am I the Queen of England or am I not? Was any woman worse served by those in attendance to her or bedevilled by such lazy good-for-nothings as I? Find me that messenger or I swear that he will spend the next few years of his life in the Tower.'

A page came hurrying out of the door, his face pale, his hands trembling. He pushed past Mistress Parry, ran across the room and had left by the other entrance almost before Andora had time to realise what was happening. She heard a low voice say something in the inner room and then the answer came, clear and impatient:

'Mistress Parry, you say! Well, ask her to come in. Perhaps she has something to tell me which has not been mislaid, forgotten or lost, as everything else in this Palace contrives to be.'

Mistress Parry went swiftly into the inner room.

'Your Majesty!' Andora heard her say. 'Mistress Andora Bland is here from Hertfordshire. You will remember that you sent for her.'

'Of course I remember I sent for her,' came the reply. 'Do you imagine I am senile? I have been expecting the wench and she has taken an unconscionable time about coming. Let me see her. Or has she got mislaid between her arrival at the Palace and her audience with me?'

'No, Your Majesty. She is here.'

'Then bring her in, bring her in. What are we waiting for?'

Andora did not wait to be called. She went through the doorway into a large room with a star-spangled gilt ceiling. It was dominated by a vast four-poster bed. A silver-topped table held an array of toilet requisites and beside it being hooked into her gown stood the Queen.

Andora did not know what she had expected but it was certainly not this vivid, colourful woman who stood in front of her. Her father had spoken so often of Elizabeth's beauty that Andora had known she would be beautiful; and yet she had not anticipated that she would be old. Yet even as Andora admitted that the Queen was old, it seemed to her that she was mistaken, for Elizabeth smiled at her and she knew that here was the most beautiful person she had ever seen in her life.

'Welcome, Andora Bland!' the Queen said, and as Andora sank in a deep curtsy at her feet she held out her exquisite, long-fingered hand in a gesture of friendliness which made the girl her slave for ever.

'Welcome to my Court!' she went on. 'Arise and let me look at you.'

Andora kissed the white hand with its heavy rings and rose to her feet. The Queen was small, but she was smaller still, and when she looked up she felt that Her Majesty towered above her and, indeed, above everyone else whom she had ever met.

The red hair ablaze with jewels, the great ruff accentuating the white, painted face, were only the frame for the Queen's eyes —

those sparkling, vivid eyes which seemed to portray every emotion one after another.

'We have been expecting you for days,' the Queen said reproachfully. 'What can have held you? I wrote to your father a month — or was it two months? — past to tell him I had need of you.'

'The roads were impassable when your letter came, Your Majesty,' Andora said. 'And also I required new clothes in which to come to Court. But now I think all our sewing was a waste of time.'

'A waste of time! How is that?' Elizabeth enquired. She spoke sharply and it seemed to Andora, in her mother's words, that Elizabeth was roaring like a lion.

'We . . . I am only a . . . country mouse, Your Majesty,' she stammered.

Elizabeth threw back her head and laughed. It was a rich laugh which seemed to echo the room.

'A country mouse!' she repeated. 'That is good, indeed, and honest of you, Mistress Bland. Few people tell the truth and I like you all the more for it. But your father's daughter shall not be allowed to feel uncomfortable at any Court of mine.'

She turned to Mistress Parry.

'Inform Lady Scudamore that the child is to have new gowns and clothes that befit her appointment and I will foot the bill. 'Tis the least I can do in return for all Sir Robert did for me.'

'That is most generous of Your Majesty,' Mistress Parry said. 'I will relay your instructions to the Mistress of the Robes.'

She glanced at Andora as she spoke as if prompting her to say thank you, but Andora stood looking at the Queen, her eyes very wide.

'Well, and what are you thinking?' Elizabeth asked.

'I was thinking,' Andora said in an awed voice, 'that for the first time I can understand why Father and so many men like him were prepared to die for Your Majesty.'

Elizabeth put out her hand and touched her shoulder.

'Thank you, my dear,' she said. 'But for the moment I require people not to die but to live for me.'

She spoke with deep sincerity, but a moment later she turned aside and was looking at herself in the big, oval mirror with its gilt frame, where it stood on her dressing-table.

'What think you, Mistress Parry?' she said. 'Does this new gown become me? Will he admire it do you think?'

'I think, Your Majesty, my Lord Essex admires everything you wear. It is the woman whom he sees, not the clothes.'

'Nonsense! Nonsense!' the Queen said, obviously not displeased at the compliment. 'Clothes are important to all women, as this child has so rightly seen. If I wore what she is wearing now, who would look at me? Do you think that their hearts would still flutter in their breasts or their breath come quickly when I appear? No! I know the effect I have on them and I am not such a fool that I do not realise it is that which sharpens their blades, encourages them to fight more fearlessly, makes them determined to bring home to me the spoils from some captured ship or the bodies of my slaughtered enemies.'

Andora was fascinated. Never had she thought that any woman could be like this. The Queen was like quicksilver, and yet she had a dignity that was unassailable. The very inflexion of her voice, every movement of those beautiful hands, had a richness, a grace and a vivacity about it which made her incomparable with anything or anybody Andora had ever imagined — let alone met — in the whole of her life.

There was a sudden knock at the door. Elizabeth turned from the mirror.

'The messenger,' she said. 'At last!'

A page came into the room and knelt on one knee to present a note on a salver of gold. Elizabeth snatched it from him. As she read what was written there, her face darkened. To Andora it was like watching a storm come up over the sea.

'So that is the answer,' she almost spat. 'Call my Lord Burleigh. Tell him to come here immediately. Inform Sir Francis Walsingham that I require his presence. And hurry! Hurry! Hurry!' she said as the page got somewhat slowly to his feet.

She flung out her arms with a sudden gesture of exasperation.

'God's death! But these delays and prevarications drive me insane,' she cried. 'Nothing can ever be done when I want it done. One must always wait, wait, when there is so little time for waiting and so much to be done.'

She paused and drew a deep breath.

'My father sent you a message, Your Majesty,' Andora said in a soft voice.

'A message?' the Queen enquired. 'And what is it?'

'He said,' Andora answered, 'that all over England men believe that next year, 1588, will be of vast importance to this country; that great events will happen which will make it the year of wonders. He begged me

27

to tell Your Majesty of this and to take heart because such prophesies, when they brew amongst the hearts of the people, invariably prove to be true.'

The Queen was very still.

'I have heard of this before,' she said in a low voice. 'I should like to believe that such prophesies will come to pass. But God helps those who help themselves, and God knows that if I did not spur these fools with whom I am surrounded into action we should soon find ourselves under the heel of Spain.'

'Your Majesty . . .' Mistress Parry began, only to be dismissed with a wave of her hand.

'Go,' Elizabeth said. 'Go, both of you. I have no further time for careless babbling. My Lord Burleigh will be here at any moment. We have things to discuss which neither of you would understand. See to the child's clothes. I wish her to be in attendance on me immediately.'

'It shall be as Your Majesty pleases,' Mistress Parry said.

She and Andora sank to the ground and then backed through the door into the antechamber. It was with a feeling almost as if she had been buffeted by a tempest that Andora found herself back in Mistress Parry's apartment.

'You are greatly honoured by Her Majesty's kindness,' Mistress Parry said. 'I have never known her to have a Maid of Honour in attendance before she has been fully instructed as to her duties.'

'If you will tell me what they are I will try to assimilate them very quickly,' Andora said.

'First I will show you your room,' Mistress Parry smiled. 'If Sir Hengist has done what he promised, your baggage should be there by now, and afterwards we must take steps to dress you as Her Majesty has commanded.'

'It is so very, very kind of her,' Andora breathed.

'There will be a reason for it,' Mistress Parry said quietly.

'A reason?' Andora questioned.

'Her Majesty does nothing without a reason,' Mistress Parry answered. 'At the moment great economies are being expected from the Court.'

She saw Andora's surprise and added:

'Her Majesty has an Army and a Navy to pay for. Her commitments are phenomenal. And yet she insists that all bills shall be met in full, especially when it is a question of paying the wages of those who serve her.'

'Then I would not wish Her Majesty to

incur further expense on my behalf,' Andora said.

'As I have said,' Mistress Parry repeated, 'if Her Majesty does so, it will be for a reason. Make quite sure that you will pay for those clothes in one way or another.'

The words were cynical, but Mistress Parry's smile as she said them was kindly and Andora could only feel a little more bewildered, a little more unsure, as she followed Mistress Parry down the passage towards the room that had been set aside for her.

It was well, if plainly furnished, and overlooked one of the many courtyards of the Palace. As Mistress Parry had anticipated, her baggage was already there and a maid in a mob cap was engaged in unpacking her boxes.

'This is Grace, who will look after you,' Mistress Parry said. 'She, too, comes from the country and finds our city ways difficult to understand.'

'I am sure we shall have much in common,' Andora replied with a smile.

'And now I will leave you,' Mistress Parry said. 'Change quickly and be ready should Her Majesty send for you. It will be your duty to be in attendance at dinner, so I will come to you half an hour before and try to tell you exactly what will be expected of you.'

'I will be ready,' Andora promised.

Wildly she wondered what she should wear, what was the least countrified of her gowns that had been made for her. She thought of the Queen's gown and realised how ludicrous she must look beside the splendour of the white satin gown embroidered with a thousand pearls or the ruff made of valuable lace and a head-dress sparkling with diamonds. Even Mistress Parry had seemed magnificent in a farthingale of deep blue velvet and an open throat ornamented with a necklace of sapphires.

'It is a very strange place, Grace,' she said, feeling more lost and lonely than she had ever felt before in her life.

'It is, indeed, Mistress,' Grace said, sitting back on her heels. 'And a powerful wicked place, too. Many's the day I regret that I came here.'

'Wicked?' Andora questioned.

'Aye, wicked. Everywhere you will find evil and sin,' Grace answered. 'Amongst the poor as well as the rich. Amongst the great nobles and the flunkeys who wait on them.'

Grace spoke with such passionate conviction that Andora could not help feeling slightly amused, even while the words frightened her. She walked across the room to open the window. As she did so she realised that she was overlooking a small courtyard which was laid out as a garden.

There was a fountain playing in the middle and the flower beds were bright with colour. At the far end was a gate which led into other gardens or perhaps a park, and as she watched she saw two men come walking through the gate and into the garden. One was tall, young and exceedingly handsome, and the other one she recognised because he was Sir Hengist Wake.

The two men were talking together as they walked towards the fountain and then suddenly they both threw back their heads and laughed. Sir Hengist said something and they both laughed again, their laughter echoing up towards her as she stood watching them, and she felt — no, indeed, she knew — that they were talking of her.

She was certain of it — as certain of it as if she could actually overhear what they were saying. And as she watched Sir Hengist's head thrown back, his eyes half closed, his whole body convulsed with merriment, she knew that she hated him with a hatred so strong and so passionate that if she could, she would do him an injury because he mocked her.

2

The Queen was dancing — floating round the room like a piece of thistledown in the arms of the tall, good-looking young man whom Andora had seen in the garden.

She had soon learned his name — the Earl of Essex. He was gay, full of high spirits, and his handsome looks, auburn hair and exquisite hands had, she learned from the other Maids-of-Honour, completely captivated the Queen.

'He is the most delightful person at Court,' Lady Mary Howard said enthusiastically. 'We all love him if the truth be told.'

'Do not let the Queen hear you,' said Mistress Elizabeth Southwell — a pretty, dark-haired girl — with a quick look over her shoulder which told Andora that though her words were light the threat was no idle one.

Andora had met many of the Maids-of-Honour before dinner. There were six of them on duty tonight, all of them young, all of them exceedingly attractive and dressed by Royal Command in shimmering gowns of white and silver. Their ruffs framed their hair which was gleaming with jewels. There were pendants round their necks while from their girdles hung a fan and a scented pomander.

If it had not been for the kindness of Lady Mary Howard, Andora would have felt sadly out of place and a complete country bumpkin beside them.

'I will lend you one of my gowns until yours are ready,' Lady Mary had said impulsively. 'We are about the same size, although I swear you are smaller in the waist than I.'

She had brought from the wardrobe in her room, a gown of white satin embroidered with silver thread and tiny pearls which had made Andora gasp with admiration.

'It is not very new as it happens,' Lady Mary said loftily. 'I have another in velvet which was only finished last week, but the skirts are very full, which makes it difficult to wear and I think you will be more comfortable in this.'

She was right. Andora found it very difficult to move gracefully in a farthingale and with skirts which had to be lifted to show her satin slippers. But the ruff, tipped with silver, was a perfect frame for her white skin and fair hair, and when she was dressed and ready to go down to the banqueting hall to attend on Her Majesty, she could not help but be thrilled by the admiration she saw in the eyes of the other Maids-of-Honour and by the compliments they paid her.

Having been an only child, Andora was inclined to feel shy with companions of her own age, but it was impossible to feel shy for long amongst the laughter, the chatter and the gaiety of Queen Elizabeth's ladies. They related the gossip of the Court and warned her about the older nobles who were susceptible to a new face and the young gallants who were always ready to play a trick on an innocent newcomer.

' 'Tis a good thing my Lord Leicester is in Holland,' Mistress Elizabeth Southwell said. 'If he were here, he would be chasing you around and you would be frightened out of your wits as to how not to offend him and, at the same time, not to let Her Majesty guess that he had even so much as thrown a glance in your direction.'

'Lord Leicester is taking a back seat now!' Eleanor Russell exclaimed. 'Just as poor Sir Walter Raleigh is having to do. There is only one person who must not smile too warmly upon you; only one person whose eye you dare not catch when there is laughter at the table; and that is . . .'

'The Earl of Essex!' they all chanted in chorus.

'Do you mean to say that the Queen is jealous?' Andora asked in amazement.

'Of course she is,' Elizabeth Southwell replied. 'When Her Majesty has a favourite, it is hands-off for everyone else.'

'He is too young for her,' Lady Mary Howard said defiantly.

'Are you going to tell her so?' someone asked.

Andora felt bewildered and a little puzzled. To her the Queen had always been a godlike figure, someone divine, of whom her father and everyone else she knew spoke in terms of fanatical admiration and abject reverence. To find that *'Gloriana'*, as they called her, was a woman with human impulses was something she had never anticipated.

And yet, as she watched the queen now dancing over the polished floor, she found it impossible not to believe there was something magical about her. Could that slender, graceful, yet proud little figure really have reigned for twenty-eight years? Could that imperious, pointed face, with its sparkling, almost hypnotic eyes under a crown of flaming red hair, belong to an ordinary woman? It was easier to credit that the

Queen was, indeed, a goddess or a witch, as her enemies preferred.

'Yes, she is very beautiful! But you are lovely! So lovely that I am afraid you will vanish into thin air,' a voice said at her ear.

Andora started and turned her head to look into two dark eyes and find they belonged to a perfect stranger.

'What is your name?' the stranger asked.

She had a moment to take in his appearance; his rich embroidered doublet; the jewel sparkling in his ear; his neatly trimmed, dark beard which matched his straight eyebrows. Then, turning her head away with an effort, she managed to say stiffly:

'I do not think we are acquainted, Sir.'

'Your pardon.'

He swept her a bow and vanished into the throng who were watching the dancing — a colourful crowd of noblemen and ladies whose doublets and gowns seemed to reflect every hue of the rainbow.

Andora felt her heart beat suddenly faster with agitation. Had she been rude? Had she, indeed, been prudish and at fault? Was it correct at Court to speak to someone to whom you had not been introduced? And what had he meant by paying her such an extravagant compliment?

37

She felt very young, small and alone. This was all too big and overwhelming. She had a longing to be back at home with her father, to hear not the music of the fiddlers but the sound of the rooks going to roost in the high trees and the soft tinkle of the brook as it ran over the small waterfall which fed the carp pool.

'Mistress Bland, may I present Lord Murton, who is exceedingly anxious to make your acquaintance?'

Andora turned round slowly. She had recognised the voice of the Mistress of the Robes, Lady Scudamore; and now, as she half expected, the gentleman being presented to her was none other than the smiling stranger who had spoken to her a few seconds earlier.

She dropped him a curtsy and as she rose, realised that Lady Scudamore had withdrawn out of earshot.

'Now may I be permitted to tell you how lovely you are?' Lord Murton enquired.

Andora did not answer and after a moment he went on:

'We have been presented to each other formally and correctly. Are the proprieties to your liking?'

'I think, my Lord, you are making fun of me,' Andora said. 'I have just arrived from the country and I am not used to Court ways.'

It seemed as if her simplicity disarmed him, for he said:

'I am sorry if I have said anything that should distress you or make you feel that I was not utterly sincere. I was speaking the truth, the whole truth, just as it came to me the moment I set eyes upon you.'

There was no doubting the sincerity in his voice, and when she looked up at him with troubled eyes she was reassured by his smile and by the kindness of his expression.

'You are feeling lost and frightened,' he said. 'I felt like that once when I first came to the Court.'

He paused and as she made no comment he went on:

'I was but seven years of age at the time and I think I cried myself to sleep every night. I wanted my home and my mother. The glittering baubles that lay around me did not compensate for the loss of my pony and my own old dog.'

'But now you like being here?' Andora said in a small voice.

'Yes, I do. Just as you will like it in time,' he said consolingly. 'You will find out that the Court of Elizabeth is the hub of the universe. It is here that everything happens, everything begins. There is never a dull moment. Couriers come and go; there is a whisper of war; another whisper of peace, of intrigue, of treachery, of loyalty and of courage. Whatever it may be, you know about it. Would you change that for a horse and a dog in an empty countryside?'

'Yes, I would at the moment,' Andora said and they both laughed.

Her laughter seemed to relieve some tension within her.

'That is better,' he said. 'Now you look happy again. No one as lovely as you should ever look anything but happy.'

She had nothing to say to that. She dropped her eyes before his and after a moment he said:

'Will you dance with me?'

'That is something of which I am also afraid,' Andora replied. 'I have learned the new dances, but I have never danced with anyone save my teacher. How shaming it will be if I make a spectacle of myself.'

As she spoke she glanced towards the Queen, who was performing some intricate steps with an assurance and a grace which made Andora feel that anything she attempted would look clumsy and ungainly in comparison.

'Shall we try in a quiet little corner where

no one will notice us?' Lord Murton said, holding out his hand.

'If you promise not to be angry with me,' Andora said smiling.

'I promise,' he replied.

She felt his fingers, warm and strong, clasp hers and quite suddenly she felt young and excited. She was no longer the quiet, unfashionable country girl who had arrived at Greenwich Palace earlier in the day. In her new gown she looked as well as, if not better than the other ladies in attendance on the Queen and she could dance as well as any of them. She was sure of it. She might not have had the experience, but she could feel it in her toes, in the rhythm throbbing in her blood and the melody running through her mind.

They joined the dancers and Andora found that with the skilful help of Lord Murton she could remember all the figures of the dance and perform them excellently. They danced for perhaps five minutes before the music came to an end. The Queen left the floor to sit, smiling and fanning herself, while Lord Essex sat beside her, a glass of wine in his hand.

It seemed rude not to speak and Andora said:

'It is hot in here, my Lord. I think perhaps

it is because there are so many tapers alight in the chandeliers. I never thought to see so many tapers alight at the same time.'

'You are right,' he agreed. 'It is stifling. Let me take you outside.'

He took her arm and led her towards one of the long windows opening from the banqueting hall on to the gardens; and just as they were about to step outside, Andora was conscious that someone else was standing behind her; someone whose presence she felt even before she turned round.

'I think I should remind you, Mistress Bland, that you are on duty tonight,' a cold voice said, and she looked up into the eyes of the man she hated and saw, as she expected, the curl of his lips above his small beard.

'Mistress Bland is well aware of her duties without your interference, Wake,' Lord Murton snapped; and Andora realised there was an old antagonism between the two men before Sir Hengist replied:

'I think it unlikely that Mistress Bland is aware that Her Majesty does not permit her Maids-of-Honour to leave the room while she still graces it with her presence.'

'Is that true?' Andora asked. 'I did not know of it.'

'And I did not know that Mistress Bland

was on duty,' Lord Murton said.

'She would be wise, even if she were not, to find someone else to show her the garden by moonlight,' Sir Hengist said with a definite sneer in his voice as he turned on his heel and walked away.

Andora stood feeling as if she had come to the very edge of a precipice and been saved at the last moment from falling over it. And yet, because she disliked her rescuer, she could not bring herself to acknowledge her gratitude to him even to herself.

'Perhaps I ought not to have danced,' she worried. 'Perhaps I should just have stood watching the Queen and waiting for Her Majesty to return to her seat.'

She looked round anxiously, only to find with a sense of relief that the other Maids-of-Honour were not grouped together but were scattered about the Great Hall talking and laughing with their friends and apparently quite at ease. But it was true, she thought, that they were all within sight. None of them had left the Hall, and how terrible it would have been for her, on this very first night, to have made the mistake of going into the garden and perhaps being fetched back by one of the attendants at Her Majesty's command.

'Forgive me! Please forgive me!' Lord

Murton was saying. 'If I had got you into trouble I should have been desperately disturbed. I would not have done such a thing for all the world.'

'You could not have known,' Andora said quickly, and yet she could not help thinking it was rather stupid of him not to have guessed that she was on duty as she was wearing white and silver, or at least to have asked before he made the suggestion that they should go into the garden.

'I think, my Lord, I should return now to Lady Scudamore,' she said.

'That means you are angry with me,' he said. 'How can I tell you how unhappy I am to have done anything which might belittle me in your eyes?'

'There is no harm done,' Andora smiled, but her thoughts were on Sir Hengist.

'I should be grateful to him,' she thought. And yet she could not help feeling that he had been glad to catch her out, to be able to rebuke her. Or had it been a chance to score over Lord Murton? Because she was curious, she could not resist her next question.

'Who is Sir Hengist Wake?' she asked.

Lord Murton raised his eyebrows.

'I thought he must be a friend of yours,' he said.

'A friend?' Andora questioned. 'No,

44

indeed. It is just that I met him today when I arrived. He . . . he laughed when my coach broke a wheel in the courtyard.'

'When you were shaken and upset — if, indeed, you were not hurt!' Lord Murton said. 'That is typical of Hengist Wake. A rough, coarse man who has come into favour simply because he is an associate of the Earl of Essex.'

'He has a special position at Court?' Andora enquired.

'A position which rests on the favour of the Earl and of the Queen,' he said. 'There are many such hangers-on. Today they are here — tomorrow they are gone.'

'I hope Sir Hengist goes,' Andora said daringly. 'He . . . he frightens me.'

'No one shall frighten you when I am there,' Lord Murton said. 'It was just unfortunate that the fellow saw that we were about to go into the garden. Otherwise we should have got there and no one would have been any the wiser.'

'Perhaps it is not usual for people even apart from Maids-of-Honour to go into the garden while the dancing is in progress?' Andora suggested.

Lord Murton looked a little uncomfortable.

'It is conventional to let the Queen go

first,' he admitted. 'But I wanted to be alone with you. I wanted to talk to you when no one could overhear. I wanted to tell you what I feel about you. Now I shall not sleep tonight because I have looked into your blue eyes and touched your little hands with mine.'

Andora took a deep breath. Never in her life had anyone spoken to her like this. Never had she imagined that a man's voice could deepen and drop almost to a whisper and yet seem to vibrate with emotion. Her heart was fluttering because of what he said and the way he was looking at her.

Quite suddenly she took fright.

'I thank you, my Lord, for the dance,' she said a little breathlessly. 'And now I must see if I am wanted. There may be duties for me to perform.'

She dropped him a curtsy and before he could stop her, slipped away to where she could see Lady Scudamore standing behind the Queen's chair. She joined her, but found the Mistress of the Robes was engaged in conversation with Lady Howard, the Keeper of the Queen's Jewels. She had nothing to do but stand in silence and when she looked back to where she had left Lord Murton he was no longer to be seen.

At the same time, the words he had

46

spoken lay warm in her heart. At least she had one friend at Court, one person who was interested in her, one person who admired her and was not ready just to find fault as apparently other people were.

She could see Sir Hengist standing in front of the great stone fireplace, a golden and jewelled goblet in his hand, his face unexpectedly serious as he listened to what an older, grey-haired man had to say.

In repose there was no doubt that he was handsome in a flamboyant manner, Andora thought. But the memory of his laughter echoing round the courtyard was still in her ears. The sneer in his voice, the curl of his lips, the amusement in his eyes — everything about him made her want to defy him, to stamp her foot at him, to toss her head, to go into the garden simply because he told her that she should not. Never had she met a man whom she detested more. And yet she had to admit that he had saved her from making a disastrous mistake.

The Queen was dancing again with the same partner, the same expression of animation, excitement and enjoyment on her face.

'She is indefatigable,' Mistress Blanche Parry groaned in a low voice. 'My feet are hurting so much that I feel I can hardly bear the pain.'

'Can you not sit down?' Andora suggested sympathetically.

'When Her Majesty is present?' Mistress Parry asked in scandalised tones. 'Goodness, child, but you have got a lot to learn. For mercy's sake ask the other ladies to instruct you in what you should and should not do, or you will be getting into a fine pickle I can see that.'

'What . . . what would happen?' Andora asked, 'if you did sit down, or someone did do something of which the Queen did not approve?'

Mistress Parry smiled a tired smile.

'You heard Her Majesty this morning,' she said, 'just before we entered her room. That was just a little squall. When there is a tempest, the whole palace shakes with the force of it.'

Andora laughed because Mistress Parry's tones were so impressive. At the same time she felt a little twinge of fear inside. She was quite certain that a tempest of the Queen's rage would leave anyone who encountered it battered and bruised and broken in spirit.

Mistress Parry moved away to speak to someone else and Andora was alone. Sir Hengist put down his goblet and walked across to her side with what she felt was an indolent and almost insulting slowness.

'You are very young,' he said in a tone of superiority that she most disliked, 'but you are woman enough to know that men will suggest many things that are best refused.'

'I must thank you, Sir, for preventing me from doing something which was not permissible,' Andora said stiffly.

'Lord Murton is not the best of guides for a Maid-of-Honour — or any other young girl,' Sir Hengist said.

'Lord Murton has apologised,' Andora retorted, 'and I have thanked you, Sir. I think there is nothing more to be said.'

'I have hurt your pride, have I not?' Sir Hengist said unexpectedly. 'Well, pride is a good thing when it is used as an armour and a protection. Be on your guard. Your innocence will not protect you in a place like this.'

'This is my first day,' Andora said coolly. 'I daresay I seem to you very raw and countrified. But I shall learn and I assure you that I shall not make the same mistake twice.'

She knew he was smiling before he spoke.

'I am delighted, Mistress Bland, that you have taken my words to heart.'

'I was not referring to your insinuations, nor shall I heed your warnings,' Andora replied. 'If I did, I would trust not one, I would go about expecting every man to behave treacherously towards me. I do not believe that people are like that. You have been so long at Court that your outlook is twisted and cynical. I think it is better to be trusting and to expect that everyone I meet is ready to be friendly.'

She spoke hastily, her words tumbling over each other because she was frightened. And yet she had said it. She had defied the cynicism in his voice and on his lips. She had stood up to him — this man of whom she was afraid.

Now she waited, her heart beating, for him to annihilate her with some sneering jibe. But, instead, he said:

'Bravo! Bravo! So you have both spirit and ideals. You are, after all, just what I expected of your father's daughter.'

'What do you mean by that?' Andora demanded.

She was past caution now. So angry, so incensed by his attitude that she could think of nothing but defying him, glaring up at him as he towered above her.

'What do I mean?' Sir Hengist repeated. 'Well, we have not much use for milksops and subservient yokels in this place. We need women of spirit and courage, women who are prepared to fight for what they believe to be right, despite the fact of their sex and their weakness.'

His words were so astonishing and the sudden sincerity in the tone of his voice so surprising that Andora was left without an answer. And then, as she longed to ask him what he meant, the Queen and Lord Essex came from the dance floor and the moment for conversation was past.

'Are you enjoying yourself, child?' the Queen asked, seeing Andora behind her chair.

'Yes, indeed, Your Majesty,' Andora replied.

'That is good,' the Queen said, and turned to the Earl of Essex. 'Robert, this is the daughter of Sir Robert Bland, of whom you have heard me speak.'

'Yes, of course,' he answered. 'Welcome to Court, Mistress Bland! I hope you find your service here agreeable and pleasant.'

His eyes lingered for a moment on the flushed, childish face as Andora dropped him a curtsy. Then the Queen's hand was on his arm and he turned to her eagerly, his eyes full of adoration, his voice young and ardent as he began a low conversation which those around could not hear.

And suddenly it seemed to Andora that there was around the two of them — the

Queen and the young man — an aura of excitement and gaiety, of youth and happiness, such as could be felt by everyone in the room. It seemed to raise the tempo, to infect everyone with a little of the emotion stirring within their hearts, until the whole place seemed a little more golden because they were there and because they were happy.

'If only time could stand still at this moment.'

Andora heard someone say the words and turned her head.

'Who was that?' she asked Mistress Parry, who had appeared again beside her.

'That was old Lord Burleigh,' Mistress Parry answered. 'He has Her Majesty's permission to retire to bed. These late nights are too much for him.'

It was many hours later before the rest of the Court had the Queen's permission to go. And then the rooms emptied only gradually because the Queen and Lord Essex were still dancing, demanding tune after tune from the fiddlers, until they too were dismissed and the card tables were brought out.

'We can go,' Mistress Parry said with a weary sigh. 'The Queen requires none of us in attendance when she settles to the cards.'

They made their curtsies to a Queen who

looked as fresh and as unfatigued as if she had just risen from her bed.

'At what time does Her Majesty retire?' Andora asked as the Maids-of-Honour shuffled down the passage, yawning and dragging their feet.

'Oh, usually long after dawn when the birds are singing,' Lady Mary Howard answered. 'It is the same every evening when Lord Essex is here. How handsome he looked tonight!'

'Oh, shut up, Mary,' Elizabeth Southwell said. 'It is too late to listen to your eulogies of Lord Essex. Besides, he is besotted with Her Majesty. Why cannot you find a man of your own?'

'They are all so dull,' Lady Mary pouted.

'I saw Lord Murton dancing with Mistress Bland,' Margaret Edgecombe said pointedly.

'Did you like him?' one of the other Maids-of-Honour enquired of Andora.

'He seemed very nice,' she answered.

'He is nice,' Elizabeth Southwell told her. 'We all like Andrew Murton, do we not, girls?'

'Yes,' the others answered in varying degrees of enthusiasm.

Andora felt pleased. She had been right, then, to like Lord Murton and Sir Hengist had been wrong. It was typical of his suspicious cynical nature to suspect that everyone was bad and everyone was wrongly intentioned.

They had reached their own corridor by now. The Maids-of-Honour said sleepy good-nights to each other and hurried into their bedchambers. Andora went to the window and pulled back the curtains. Outside the dawn was coming up over the rooftops of the Palace, the stars were still glittering in the darkness of the sky but there was just the faint glow of the approaching sun.

She stopped and looked at it. What a lot had happened since dawn the day before. It seemed as if an eternity had passed since she had left home, yet here she was, a Maid-of-Honour to the most famous and the most feared Queen in all the world.

She had expected such an experience to be glorious, exciting and awe-inspiring. She had not expected it to be so full of so many trivial emotions, so many hates and loves, so many anxieties and apprehensions.

And even as she thought of all she had felt during the day, she heard footsteps below. Almost as if she had expected to see him, she saw Sir Hengist walking along the paved path of the courtyard, going, she suspected, to another wing of the Palace where his lodgings must be situated.

He was walking bare-headed, one hand holding his sword and the other at his belt. He walked slowly, as a man deep in thought, and she watched him as if fascinated, wondering what he was thinking, half expecting that his laughter would ring out and awaken the sleeping Palace.

'I hate him!' she thought. Strange that one should hate a man whom one had met such a short time ago. Strange that such hatred should seem to animate her whole body, making her fingers clench and her breath seem to come a little quicker.

And then, as if her thoughts reached him and her very hatred leapt to halt his footsteps, he stopped suddenly, turned and looked upward. The pale light in the sky was on Andora's face, her fair head was silhouetted against the darkness of the room behind her.

They looked at each other. She felt — though it was impossible to be sure — that their eyes met, defiantly and antagonistically, piercing even the darkness which divided them.

And then he bowed to her — a magnificent Court bow in which his strong body bent from the waist. But as he raised himself he lifted his arm and waved, and his voice, filled with laughter, rang out to echo round the sleeping courtyard.

'Good night, Andora! Sleep well!'

'Andora' indeed! The impertinence of it made Andora slam the window so violently that she almost dislodged the diamond panes of glass. Then she pulled the curtains as if in doing so she shut him out of her life.

Andora! How dared he address her by her Christian name? Tomorrow, if she got the chance, she would tell him exactly what she thought of such impertinence!

3

The next day Andora found the Court and the Palace even more complex than she had found them the day before. It was not surprising that it was bewildering to a girl who had until now lived a simple life in the country.

In front of it smooth green lawns ran down to the Thames where the tall ships could be seen passing up and down the chief road of the kingdom. The great Palace sprawled over acres of ground but behind the grey walls were myriads of dark courtyards and twisting passages.

Here lodged fifteen hundred people, ranging from high and noble officials down to kitchen menials. Many of the servants were in private employ, and Andora realised with a sinking heart that she would be expected to recognise the colourful liveries which distinguished the retinue of each employer of noble birth. But, at the same time, she must not confuse them with the gentlemen ushers who were also vividly and colourfully dressed.

She found also that there were a score or
so more ladies in attendance on the Queen
than she had already met and that most of
the Maids-of-Honour had been sent to
Court by their parents to finish their educa-
tion.

It was like living in a huge town all housed
in one vast building; and already she was beginning to sense some of the jealousies, en-
mities and feuds which automatically spring
up amongst people confined in such close
quarters.

The six Maids-of-Honour whom she had
met the night before were kind and helpful
and for this Andora was grateful. They
showed her how to curtsy. They attempted
to instruct her in the depth and formality of
the greeting she should give to the different
Court officials. They also tried to give her a
potted history of the more important people
surrounding the Queen, but here Andora
shut her ears and was not prepared to listen.

It was difficult enough to learn all that
was required of her without assimilating
ready-made opinions about those whom she
would encounter during her service on the
Queen.

One thing she realised all too quickly —
she was lamentably ignorant.

'The Queen can carry on conversations with perfect ease in Latin, French and Italian,' Lady Howard, the Keeper of the Queen's Jewels, told her. 'She also appears to know everything that happens, not only in this kingdom but over the whole of Europe. If you wish to please her, you must try to have a knowledge of the war in the Netherlands, the strange behaviour of the King of France and the ailing health of His Majesty of Spain.'

'But how can one know all these things?' Andora asked in amazement.

'One cannot,' Lady Howard replied. 'But if you listen to the gentlemen, one can pick up enough to incite Her Majesty to do the talking.'

Her eyes twinkled as she said it and Andora began to think that perhaps the scholarship expected of her was not so formidable as she had at first feared.

'Andora already has a gentleman who will tell her the latest gossip in the Council Chamber,' a pretty Maid-of-Honour from Yorkshire said teasingly.

'Oh, yes, we all saw how attentive Lord Murton was last night,' Elizabeth Southwell remarked.

Andora felt herself blushing.

'It was kind of him to speak to me when I

59

knew no one else,' she said demurely.

'Kind!' Mary Radcliffe exclaimed. 'Lord Murton is not kind! He just has an eye for a pretty girl. And there is no doubt about it, Andora, you are a dangerous rival for us to have in our midst.'

Andora blushed again and tried to change the conversation, but they teased her still further when a bouquet of rosebuds was brought to the room a little while later by a page wearing Lord Murton's livery.

'He is serious about you, there is no doubt about that!' one of the girls exclaimed, while Andora, crimson with embarrassment, escaped to her own bed chamber, hiding in her hand the note which had accompanied the flowers.

When she was alone, she opened it. It was very short — only a few lines.

My heart will not rest until I see you again. Meet me in the garden at noon when Her Majesty will not require your services.

Murton

Andora read it carefully, then tore it into small pieces and dropped it into her waste-paper basket. She had no intention of going — that she knew would be a very foolish thing to do. At the same time it was not unpleasant to know that one man at least found her attractive and desired her company.

At noon she was standing being fitted into one of the new gowns that the Queen had ordered for her; but she could not help wondering whether Lord Murton was really waiting for her in the garden, perhaps watching the entrance impatiently or walking up and down and growing gradually angry because she did not appear.

She had learned why the Queen did not require her services. Her Majesty had gone riding in the woods with the Earl of Essex.

'She does not ask us to accompany her,' Lady Howard said. 'Personally I would welcome the chance.'

'Not only because you like riding,' someone taunted her, 'but because we know whom else besides Her Majesty you admire on a horse.'

'You have to admit he looks magnificent,' Lady Mary said defiantly.

'All the same, he would not notice you even if you were there,' Lady Elizabeth Southwell said crushingly. 'Forget him. There are lots of other good-looking young men at Court.'

Lady Mary walked angrily to the window

to stare with unseeing eyes at the sun-kissed river.

'Love! Love!' Elizabeth Trentham said theatrically. 'How I pray that I remain heart-whole while I am here!'

'Do you think love brings unhappiness?' Andora asked timidly.

'It does here!' Elizabeth replied. 'Look at Mary, crying into her pillow and lying awake over a man who has eyes only for the Queen. Look at Frances, the girl you see sewing in the corner. She was crazed with love last year for the Earl of Leicester and he flirted with her until the Queen got angry and gave them both such a reprimand that he did not dare speak to her again. So all Frances has got now is a broken heart and a lot of black looks from the Queen, who has not yet forgiven her.'

'But surely there must be people in the Palace who fall in love and get married?' Andora suggested.

'Yes, of course,' Elizabeth Trentham said. 'But then they go away. They retire to live in the country and we seldom hear of them again.'

'Would you like that?' Andora asked.

'I am not sure,' Elizabeth answered. 'It is so exciting being here, so gay. There are so many things to do, so many people to meet.

And, yet, I do not know. I expect one day I shall get married — and then I must be prepared to give it all up.'

Andora kept her counsel and did not say what she herself would prefer; but already behind the glitter and the brilliance of the Court, she was beginning to find heartaches and unhappiness. Things she had never anticipated.

When the Queen returned from riding, Andora and three other Maids-of-Honour were waiting in the inner courtyard to escort Her Majesty into the Palace, and if she wished it, to help her change her gown. The sunshine was warm as they waited and Andora began to feel sleepy and ceased to listen to the whispering exchange of gossip which went on between the other girls.

Suddenly through the gateway came the first sign of the glittering cavalcade that had accompanied Elizabeth into the woods. Instantly all feeling of drowsiness was gone. The very air seemed to sharpen and the sunshine brighten. The sentries sprang to attention; there was the clatter of horses' hoofs on the cobbles, the jingle of silver bridles.

Then Elizabeth herself appeared, perched upon a white horse bedecked in crimson harness. Her cheeks were flushed from the exercise, her eyes were glittering, and she looked young, excited and happy as she talked animatedly to the tall, good-looking young man at her side.

He was bending towards her, his dark, dreamy eyes held by hers, and Andora was able to notice again how strongly built he was and yet how graceful with a high forehead and a sensitive, tender mouth.

'It is not surprising she loves him,' she thought involuntarily, and then forgot Lord Essex in her admiration of the Queen. Clad in a gown of white velvet, she might have been ready to sit for her portrait rather than have just been enjoying a canter with her gentlemen.

Lord Essex sprang from his horse to help her dismount and it seemed to Andora that her fingers lingered in his rather longer than was necessary and that their eyes seemed to be held by each other for one ecstatic moment before the Queen released herself and turned to her Maids-of-Honour.

'What pale faces I see around me!' she exclaimed. 'You should take more exercise, ladies. It would become you vastly. And, now, who is waiting to see me? For I am sure that I must pay for my brief enjoyment by some hard work.'

She looked to the top of the steps as she

spoke and Andora saw that Sir Francis Walsingham was waiting there, serious and sombre looking. It was difficult to think that he had anything but bad news to tell her, but the Queen held out her hand to him with a smile and he bent to kiss it with a courtly grace.

'The Ambassadors, Your Majesty, crave an audience,' he said loudly enough for Andora to hear his words.

'Then we must not keep them waiting,' Elizabeth replied.

She walked up the steps and through the great, stone doorway into the darkness of the passage. It seemed to Andora following behind that they were led by a rainbow, for the sparkle, beauty and colour of the Queen, seemed to light the passage and her voice, high and amused, seemed to warm even the grey stones on which they walked.

To watch the Queen receive the Ambassadors from other countries was a lesson in diplomacy. She was charming, severe, a little frigid, enthusiastic, complimentary, in a manner which left them all gasping, which promised nothing and yet raised their hopes almost to fever point.

She took one to see the gardens from the window and while the others seethed with jealousy she turned about and showed another her pictures. She conversed in several languages; and then, as Andora watched, fascinated by the display of erudition, charm and brilliance, she heard a voice at her own shoulder whisper:

'Have you learned so quickly how to be cruel by being kind?'

She turned her head swiftly to find Lord Murton beside her. He was splendidly dressed and she realised that he had joined the ranks of gentlemen in attendance. She did not answer and after a moment he went on:

'Sir Christopher Haddon says that the Queen does fish for men's souls with so sweet a bait that none can escape her network. You fish for men's hearts — and already mine is in your net.'

'Hush!'

Andora hardly breathed the word for she was afraid that the Queen would hear Lord Murton talking and she had already been instructed that those in attendance did not converse when Her Majesty was speaking.

'She will not hear us,' Lord Murton said soothingly, and that was true enough for the Queen had walked across the long room to show the Ambassador with whom she was speaking at that moment something that was written in a book that she drew from one of the shelves.

'But, my Lord, you embarrass me,' Andora said.

'And you make me unhappy,' he answered. 'Why did you not come? I waited and waited in the hot sun, not believing that anyone could be so cruel and hard-hearted.'

'Did you really believe that I should do such a thing?' Andora asked. 'I may be simple but not as simple as that, my Lord.'

'I love you, Andora. Have you not learned that a man in love will risk anything to see the object of his affections?'

'You cannot love anyone whom you have known for so short a time,' Andora said crushingly.

'That is not true,' Lord Murton said. 'I fell in love with you the moment I saw that sweet little, serious face of yours, those frightened eyes, those trembling lips. Andora, let me look after you and protect you.'

'The only person from whom I need protection is yourself, my Lord,' Andora said.

She must have raised her voice a little for Mistress Parry turned her head and looked round with a frown to see who was speaking, and several of the gentlemen also turned.

Frightened by what she had done Andora

moved from Lord Murton's side and crossed behind the Queen's empty chair to stand by Lady Mary Howard. The elder girl gave her a faint smile but said nothing and to Andora's relief the Queen came walking back towards them so there was no possibility of further conversation with anyone.

As soon as the audience was finished, Lord Essex was at the Queen's side again; and now the conversation became general and Andora realised with a little sinking of her heart that Lord Murton was seeking her out.

'I must talk with you. It is agony to see you only in a crowd when there is so much that I have to say which can only be said when we are alone.'

'I think, my Lord, that you will get me a bad reputation,' Andora said. 'I beg of you, leave me alone. Perhaps when I have been here longer it will be easier to make friends, but at the moment I wish only to learn my duties and try to understand a little of the ceremonial in which I have to take my place.'

'You are cruel and unkind,' he said accusingly, but he moved away from her and stood at the other side of the room watching her, his eyes on her face so that she was conscious of him the whole time.

She was wondering despairingly what she could do about such an impetuous suitor when one of the Ushers bowed before her and said:

'My Lord Burleigh wishes to see you, Mistress Bland.'

'Lord Burleigh!' Andora ejaculated.

'Yes, indeed. His Lordship was well acquainted with your father and I have a suspicion that he wishes to welcome you to the Palace.'

'That is indeed kind of him,' Andora said. 'I must ask Mistress Parry if I may accompany you.'

She asked permission from the Mistress of the Robes who gave it saying:

'You are honoured. There are not many Maids-of-Honour who are welcomed by the Lord Chancellor.'

Andora followed the gentleman who had come for her down passages, twisting and turning until they came to another part of the Palace where Lord Burleigh had his rooms and where she knew much of the business of the nation was transacted.

'Wait here a moment,' the Usher said when they approached a door heavily carved and dark with age.

He went inside leaving Andora a little apprehensive. She thought how often she had heard her father tell of the brilliance of Lord Burleigh; how often she had been told that he was the stalwart pillar on which the State rested and on whom even Elizabeth herself relied.

The Usher reappeared and opened the door.

'His Lordship will see you,' he said.

Feeling suddenly very small and insignificant, Andora slipped through the opening and heard the door close behind her. She was in a big, square room, dark because it was lined with books, and across the huge desk which was facing her she saw Lord Burleigh.

She recognised him from her father's description — the square, greying beard, the shrewd penetrating eyes, the dark robes which she knew hid the swollen legs which gave the ageing man incessant twinges of agony.

Old he might be, but his voice was clear and forceful as he spoke her name.

'Mistress Andora Bland,' he said.

Andora sank down in a curtsy.

'It is a great honour to meet you, my Lord,' she said.

'I would not allow my old friend's daughter to go unwelcomed,' he said and rose to his feet, a little flicker of pain narrowing his eyes and sharpening his lips before he held out his hand to her.

And as Andora rose she saw that there were two other men in the room — Sir Francis Walsingham and, to her astonishment, Sir Hengist Wake. Her eyes flickered towards him and then she realised that he was standing in the background, as it were, with an expression on his face that she could not fathom, but one which she felt instinctively she disliked.

She curtsied to Sir Francis and then both the elder men resumed their seats at the desk and Lord Burleigh indicated a chair in front of it.

'Please be seated, Andora,' he said. 'You must forgive me if I speak in what may seem a familiar manner, but I was with your father when he chose your name and I have heard him talk of you since you were but a baby.'

'It is a compliment that your Lordship should remember my name,' Andora said politely.

'Your father is well?' Lord Burleigh enquired.

'As well as he ever is,' Andora replied. 'It is two years now since he has been able to leave his bed; but he sleeps on the ground floor so that the business of the estate may

71

be brought to him, and it keeps him interested and even, at times, makes him forget the pain.'

'An honourable man and a loyal servant of Her Majesty,' Lord Burleigh said.

There was a pause and Andora wondered what she should say; but she had the feeling that all this conversation was but a prelude to something else. Why was Sir Hengist here? she wondered. And why had Lord Burleigh made no mention of him or even introduced them?

She saw Sir Francis Walsingham glance at Lord Burleigh; and then, after looking down at the papers before him as if they contained something to prompt his words, Lord Burleigh said:

'I believe, Andora, that you speak Spanish.'

The remark was unexpected and Andora paused before she replied:

'Yes, indeed, my Lord. It may seem a strange accomplishment, but when my father was a prisoner he was befriended by a man and his wife who were subsequently captured when my father was rescued. My father made himself responsible for them and they came to live at our house and the woman became my nurse. I learned from her to speak the Spanish tongue.'

'You have not spoken of this to anyone at Court?' Lord Burleigh asked.

'No, indeed,' Andora answered. 'No one asked me and I feel that at the moment it is not something of which one should be particularly proud.'

'No, of course,' Sir Francis interposed a little heavily. 'At the same time, it might be useful.'

'Useful?'

Andora raised her eyebrows.

'You speak French, too, I understand,' Lord Burleigh went on.

'A little,' Andora admitted, 'but only what I have learned from books. I have never had the opportunity of conversing with a native of France.'

'That is what your father told me,' Lord Burleigh said.

'My father!' Andora ejaculated. 'I am afraid I do not understand, my Lord.'

Lord Burleigh bent forward across the desk.

'Tell me, Andora,' he said, 'have you any idea why you are here?'

Andora looked from him to Sir Francis Walsingham.

'I . . . I understood that Her Majesty asked for me to come,' she replied. 'I thought that she was in need of a Maid-of-Honour.'

Lord Burleigh smiled.

'Her Majesty has plenty of those,' he said. 'And plenty more eager to sample the gaieties of Court. No, Andora, that was ostensibly the reason for which you have come to Greenwich — but there is much more to it than that.'

'But what?' Andora enquired. 'I must be very dense.'

'Explain to the girl,' Sir Francis Walsingham said. 'Her father obviously obeyed your instructions, my Lord, and said nothing.'

'It was safer that way,' Lord Burleigh said. 'Now, Andora, let me explain to you.'

Andora clasped her hands together, her heart beating quickly. This was all so unexpected, something she had not anticipated in any way. Then suddenly she raised her eyes and saw that Sir Hengist, standing in the shadows, was watching her and she knew quite clearly and distinctly that he disapproved.

'You well know,' she heard Lord Burleigh say, 'the valiant and invaluable service your father has given to Her Majesty. I think it broke his heart when he could serve her no longer and he has written to me often regretting that he had no son to carry on where he left off. But the Sovereign is not always served by the sword. There are other ways — and that is why your father has sent you here.'

'To do something special?' Andora asked.

'To do anything that might be required,' Lord Burleigh answered.

'But, of course, I am only too willing,' Andora said, at the same time feeling a little bewildered. What were they going to ask of her?

'I think your father must have thought of this many years ago,' Lord Burleigh said. 'Perhaps even while he was still hoping that he would have a son. It was for that reason he had you instructed in the Spanish tongue. He knew a little Spanish himself and he has often said to me how useful it had proved to him that he was able to converse with his prisoners without an interpreter, or in helping him to find his way in Spanish territory.'

'I recall now how insistent my father was that I should be very fluent,' Andora said. 'I used to think it strange that he should wish me to learn the language of our enemies.'

'But now you are going to see how wise he was,' Sir Francis said.

'What can I do?' Andora asked simply.

She saw a glance pass between the two

elderly men as if they were pleased at her question.

'I think I had better explain,' Lord Burleigh said. 'You see, Andora, things are often very difficult for Her Majesty because she is never quite certain whom she can trust.'

He saw Andora's eyes widen and he went on:

'Let me put this even more frankly. There are traitors even in the very midst of us.'

'Oh, no!' Andora exclaimed impulsively. 'That cannot be true!'

'Alas, we have at the moment a very certain knowledge of it,' Lord Burleigh replied. 'You will recall that in the February of this year Mary Queen of Scots lost her head on the block.'

'Yes, I remember,' Andora said in a low voice, remembering how many people had been shocked when the news had reached the country.

'After the axe had fallen,' Lord Burleigh went on, 'a courier left immediately to inform our Ambassador in Paris. He travelled as swiftly and as secretly as it was humanly possible to do, but before he could break the news to Sir Edward Stafford, the Spanish Ambassador to the Court of the King of France, Don Bernardino de

Mendoza, had already learned of Queen Mary's death.'

'But, surely, that would be impossible!' Andora exclaimed.

'That is what we thought,' Lord Burleigh replied. 'But this is not the only news that has reached Don Bernardino more quickly than our couriers have reached our own Ambassador, the English Resident. So there is only one conclusion that Sir Francis and I can draw from this.'

'And what is that?' Andora enquired.

'It is that there is someone at Court, someone near to the Queen's own person, who is in league with Spain.'

'A traitor!'

Andora hardly breathed the words.

'Exactly,' Lord Burleigh said. 'And if this is true, how dangerous it must be for Her Majesty! Her very person may be threatened.'

'But, surely, surely you have a suspicion of who it might be?' Andora asked.

Lord Burleigh spread out his long, white fingers.

'How?' he asked. 'It might be me; it might be Sir Francis. It might be anyone; but in fact it must be someone so utterly and completely English that we have never for one moment suspected him or her. And yet his heart has turned against our lawful Queen and he seeks once more to place a Catholic on the Throne of England.'

'You are sure of this? Absolutely sure?' Andora asked.

'Sir Francis and I have not made up our minds entirely on this score,' Lord Burleigh replied. 'If it had been just one piece of news reaching Don Bernardino, we should have thought it strange but not in any way sensational. But this is continual — that is the right word, Andora, continual. Our Ambassador complains almost daily that he is often the last person in the French Court to know some piece of news from England.'

'Who can it be?' Andora asked.

'We have looked over everyone in close attendance on Her Majesty; we have tried to find out if they have any foreign contacts, if they send couriers. In fact we have thought of everything, but always our investigations come to a dead end and we learn nothing. It was at that point that your father's letter arrived.'

'My father wrote to you?' Andora enquired.

Lord Burleigh nodded.

'Yes, he wrote suggesting that because you could speak Spanish you might be of service to Her Majesty. I think perhaps he knew by instinct that we were worried, for it could not have been anything anyone had said to him.'

'Sometimes we have accused my father of being clairvoyant,' Andora smiled. 'He seems to know in advance what will happen.'

'Then my worry and anxiety must have flown over the miles that lie between us so that he knew we had need of his help,' Lord Burleigh smiled.

'But, how can I help you?' Andora asked. 'It is not likely that people will be speaking Spanish here in Greenwich Palace.'

'Who knows?' Lord Burleigh questioned. 'We have no idea what language they may speak. But we have tried everything else — in fact, Andora, you are our last hope.'

'But how shall I begin? For what shall I seek?'

'If I could tell you that,' Lord Burleigh replied, 'we might be half-way to solving the problem for ourselves. We can only ask you to watch and listen. You are new. You came here without the least suspicion that you might be concerned with anything other than serving Her Majesty as a Maid-of-Honour.'

He pulled at his grey beard.

'Perhaps you will pick up some careless

remark,' he went on. 'Perhaps, because you are young and unused to Court life, you will notice something which has escaped us simply because we are familiar with it. We do not know. We only know that we are desperate and we must clutch at anything that may help us at this moment.'

'It seems impossible,' Andora said. 'And how shall I hear anything, moving amongst the Maids-of-Honour?'

'We can tell you nothing more than we have told you already,' Lord Burleigh replied. 'All we have done is to ask you to come here, and we have worked out a certain formula which may or may not be of help.'

'A formula?' Andora questioned.

'Yes,' Lord Burleigh answered, 'for you must not be seen talking to me or to Sir Francis Walsingham. It is understandable that I should have sent for you today because your father is an old friend of mine. But having welcomed you to the Palace I shall, of course, ignore you in future, just as I ignore all those other charming young ladies who flutter around Her Majesty like butterflies round a flower.'

'Then how . . . ?' Andora began, only to be silenced by the raising of Lord Burleigh's hand.

'This is what we have arranged amongst ourselves,' he said. 'The Queen, as you know, is in constant communication with my Lord Essex. When she sends him a note, it is usually conveyed by one of her Maids-of-Honour to one of the Earl's gentlemen. We have chosen Sir Hengist Wake — whom you see here — to receive from you such letters as the Queen may wish to send to Lord Essex. When you give him these, you will tell him anything that excites your suspicion or anything which appears to need investigating.'

At the name of Sir Hengist, Andora had looked up at him. His eyebrows were almost meeting across his forehead and his lips were not smiling but tightly pressed together. Lord Burleigh followed her gaze and said:

'I think I should tell you, Andora, that Sir Hengist does not approve of this plan. He thinks you are too young and too inexperienced for such intrigue.'

'She is too young!' Sir Hengist said, speaking for the first time since Andora had entered the room. 'A child from the country; a child unused to the machinations of Court life. How can she help?'

The scorn in his voice made Andora stiffen her back and put up her chin. She gave Sir Hengist one look of enmity and turning to Lord Burleigh said quickly:

'I am very honoured and gratified, my Lord, that you should ask my help in the service of our gracious Queen. I swear to you that I will do all in my power to seek out these traitors, whoever they may be. I can only pray that I may have the privilege of serving Her Majesty, even as my father has done.'

Lord Burleigh smiled at her.

'I hoped, indeed, that you would say that,' he said. 'But be careful, Andora. Remember these things are not undertaken lightly nor, indeed, will Her Majesty's enemies be gentle or kind should you be instrumental in discovering them. A cornered rat will fight, and fight with every weapon in his power.'

'I am not afraid of danger for myself,' Andora said quickly.

'What can she know about it?' Sir Hengist sneered. 'She has listened to brave deeds recounted by her father and thinks that she can fight the Spanish single-handed. Fairytales of the nursery! This is reality and she is more likely to find her throat slit or her eyes gouged out in some dark passage than to bring us anything which will be of the least consequence.'

'That is for his Lordship to judge,' Andora said angrily. Her eyes now met Sir Hengist's defiantly and she saw, as she suspected, his lips curl derisively as if he thought her anger childish and ridiculous.

She turned again to Lord Burleigh, putting both her hands on the desk in her eagerness.

'Let me try, my Lord,' she said. 'I swear to you I will be careful and not foolhardy, but I will suspect everyone. If, indeed, Her Majesty's life is in danger, then we must be ready to prevent an attack from wherever it comes.'

'She has got the right idea,' Sir Francis Walsingham approved with a note of surprise in his voice.

'You realise, Andora, that we cannot help you?' Lord Burleigh asked. 'You will be alone on this. You can tell only Sir Hengist and no one else. The only thing we can ensure is that no one shall suspect you. If you carry Her Majesty's letters there will be nothing unusual in her choosing you from among her ladies. She often takes a fancy to a new face.'

'I will do everything in my power to find the traitor,' Andora said, and it was as if she made a vow and she thought that her voice seemed to ring round the room.

'That is settled then,' Sir Francis
Walsingham said.

'Yes, it is settled,' Lord Burleigh agreed.

'Thank you, Andora. You have proved, as
I expected, to be your father's daughter. He
will be proud of you, I do not doubt it.'

Realising that she was dismissed, Andora
rose to her feet. She curtsied first to Lord
Burleigh and then to Sir Francis.

'Good-bye, my child,' Lord Burleigh
said.

Andora walked towards the door. Deliberately she did not look at Sir Hengist; deliberately she ignored him even when he
reached the door before her to open it. She
saw his hand go out towards the latch and
then he said in a low voice which only she
could hear:

'For God's sake do not go looking for
trouble. You have no idea what you have
undertaken.'

His words stung her and she raised her
eyes to his.

'You, of course, would not understand,
but I am a soldier's daughter,' she retorted,
her tone defiant, her words contriving to be
insulting.

She expected him to smile and scorn her,
but his expression was serious as without
another word he opened the door and let

her pass through. She stepped out into the passage and found the Usher waiting for her, ready to escort her back.

'You are honoured,' he said cheerily as she joined him again. 'What do you think of Lord Burleigh?'

'He is a very great man,' Andora replied.

'At the same time he is old,' the Usher said. 'It does not give the young ones at Court a chance when the old ones cling to their posts for so long. Things will be better now Lord Essex has become Master of the Horse. Perhaps more appointments will be given to us younger men.'

Andora smiled politely, feeling there was nothing she could contribute to the conversation which would not seem contradictory.

'Sir Hengist was in there, was he not?' the Usher asked.

'Yes, he was.'

Andora felt it would seem strange if she did not answer this question.

'What do you think of him?' the Usher enquired.

'I think he is typical of the sort of young man one expects to find lounging lazily about a Palace,' Andora answered.

She had not meant to say anything so defamatory but somehow the words seemed to come to her lips, to burst out before she could control them. The Usher looked surprised.

'But Sir Hengist has not been here long,' he said. 'He arrived back at the beginning of the year with Sir Francis Drake and wanted to accompany him when he left again in April, but the Queen insisted on his staying behind.'

'He was with Sir Francis Drake!'

Andora stopped dead and stared at the voluble young Usher.

'Yes, of course, did you not know? He was with him in the Caribbean. He came back covered with glory. Oh, he is no smooth courtier — not Sir Hengist. Is that what you thought of him?'

He threw back his head and laughed. Andora felt the colour ebbing from her cheeks. How she had misjudged Sir Hengist, she thought. He was a friend of Francis Drake — a man who was a hero to the whole nation.

And, yet, how was she to have known? How could she find him anything but detestable considering the way he treated her? And then her last taunt came back to her mind and made her feel uncomfortable.

'You, of course, would not understand, but I am a soldier's daughter,' she had said.

But if he had understood — and, of

course, he must have done, seeing who he was — then why had he been so against her trying to serve the Queen in the only way she could? Why? Why?

The question persisted with Andora long after she had been taken back to the audience chamber. Why? Why?

4

Andora wandered through the garden in the sunshine. It was the second time she had been there this day. Whatever time they went to bed the Maids-of-Honour had to be up next morning at six o'clock to attend the Queen as she walked in the gardens.

It was Her Majesty's hour of relaxation before the Ministers arrived to consult her about State affairs. Andora, therefore, had already seen the green, dew-spangled lawns broken by trim flower beds; the fantastically clipped bushes and the wealth of colour in the shrubs and flowering trees which scented the air with their fragrance and vied with the Queen's jewels in beauty and colour.

Now it was after midday, the sun was high and the rest of the Maids-of-Honour were resting or sewing in their rooms. But the Queen, before she dismissed them, had said:

'I have a note for my Lord Essex. Which of you, I wonder, will be my messenger?'

She had looked round at the young faces gazing attentively at her and added with a little laugh:

'I might almost say, my messenger of love.'

Then before anyone could speak or volunteer she added:

'I think I will send my little country mouse. She is not yet spoiled by the intrigues and gossip of the Court and will therefore be less likely to linger by the way or — look for trouble.'

It seemed to Andora that for a moment the Queen's eyes rested on Mary Howard's pretty, oval face before she went on:

'Take this note, Andora Bland. Give it to one of the gentlemen who attend his Lordship — Sir Hengist Wake would be the safest, I think — and tell him to place it in my Lord Essex's hand and none other's.'

It was cleverly done, Andora thought. Her decision on who should carry the note was not likely to cause jealousy amongst the other Maids-of-Honour, while only the Queen and she knew there was another reason why she had been chosen.

Andora had lain awake all night worrying over the part she had to play and worrying, too, about her words to Sir Hengist. As she thought of what she had said and the manner in which she had said it, she could feel the colour rise again and again in her face, burning there as evidence of her shame and humiliation at having made such a mistake about him.

She had imagined — all too easily because she wished to disparage him — that he was but a courtier. One of the many young men who hung about the Palace, anxious for any pickings that were available from the Royal favour, and doing nothing but bedeck themselves in their finery, spending their evenings attending banquets and many hours of the day at the card tables.

How wrong she had been. Sir Hengist had served with Sir Francis Drake — the man who was the hero of England, whose reputation was such that he invested anyone he knew or who sailed with him with the aura of his own bravery and splendour.

'Fool, fool that I was,' Andora told herself in the darkness, 'not to have discovered more about him before I insulted him.'

It was easy to remember that he had insulted her first. And yet now that she looked back on it, she could not help feeling that perhaps the spectacle of the coach collapsing on the cobbles had caused justifiable merriment.

She hated him from the moment his

laughter had rung out, and yet that was no excuse for disparaging his courage.

'Never be unjust to any man.'

How often had her father said that to her as he had recounted his adventures in the Queen's service?

'I have fought many enemies,' he would go on, 'I have killed men and I have denounced them. But always, little Andora, my cause has been just. I have fought for what was right, for what was true.'

As she had tossed on her narrow bed, Andora thought that her cause had not been just and true in her war with Sir Hengist. It had been personal and petty, both things for which she despised herself.

'I must apologise to him,' she thought and knew it was the least she could do. And yet the thought of it made her feet lag and her heart beat suffocatingly fast as at last she saw him approaching. He was coming towards her through an archway of roses, his black velvet doublet slashed with silver and an impudent orange feather floating in the breeze from his velvet hat, which was tilted over his right eye.

The rose garden was gay with blossom. It was small and surrounded by high box hedges which prevented those who lingered there from being overlooked. Andora sank down in a curtsy which was lower than usual because she felt humble and a little ashamed of herself.

'Your servant, Mistress Bland,' Sir Hengist said, making his usual extravagant bow.

Andora rose and looked up at him. Her face was a little paler than usual and her fingers trembled as she held out the Queen's note with its heavy seal.

'Did Her Majesty play her part well?' Sir Hengist asked with a hint of laughter in his voice. 'It was difficult to see why you should be sent on such an errand when usually it is the duty of Mary Howard or Bridget Manners to convey these *billets-doux*.'

'Her Majesty said that as I was new to the Court I should not be steeped in its intrigues and gossip and that was why she had chosen me.'

'The little country mouse, eh?' Sir Hengist questioned.

Andora felt the blush rise in her cheeks. She had hoped that he had not heard this description of her which, though she had given it to herself, she felt now was not particularly complimentary.

She did not answer and then after a moment he said:

'But I will not tease you. I have a note for

92

you to take back to Her Majesty.'

He handed it to her with a little flourish and then, looking at her downcast eyes, said:

'Have you nothing else to tell me?'

'Nothing else?' Andora asked, startled, feeling that he must be clairvoyant if he realised that she was searching for the words in which to frame her apology.

And then as she saw the twinkle in his eyes she realised that he was speaking of very different matters.

'I have not discovered anything yet, Sir,' she said defensively, 'if that is what you mean.'

'I did not think you had,' he answered. 'And I assure you that it is very unlikely that you ever will. Forget it, child. They will think none the worse of you if you find no dastardly plot hatching in the Maids-of-Honour's room, and there are other people to deal with what happens in the rest of the Palace.'

'I shall do my duty as I find it,' Andora said stiffly.

'Your duty, yes,' Sir Hengist agreed. 'But do not look for danger. I assure you that when you find it, it is often very unpleasant.'

'You have had experience of such things,' Andora said in a low voice. 'And, please, there is something I wish to say to you.'

Her tone was low, but she thought that he was suddenly alert, listening intently to what she had to say.

'What is it?' he asked.

'I . . . I wish to . . . apologise,' Andora stammered, speaking with difficulty for the words seemed to choke her. 'I should n . . . not have spoken to you . . . the way I did. But I . . . I did not know that . . . you served in the Caribbean or that you were anything . . . but just a gentleman of the Court.'

'And now that you do know,' Sir Hengist said, and she realised that the gay, mocking note had returned to his voice, 'your whole opinion of me has doubtless changed.'

'Yes . . . I mean n . . . no,' Andora answered, finding herself at a loss for words.

'I am, indeed, honoured that you should have thought of me at all,' Sir Hengist said. 'But I assure you that you owe me no apology. I am, at this moment, nothing but a gentleman of the Court. I wished to sail with Drake and was not permitted to do so. I must therefore kick my heels with all the other wasters and sycophants.'

'They would not let you go?' Andora said, startled by the bitterness in his voice, the sudden grimness of the expression on his face.

'No, my pleadings were refused,' he said abruptly. 'So you need not apologise. I am exactly what you thought me.'

'No, no,' Andora protested. 'You do not understand. I thought you had never done anything. Oh, it was presumptuous of me, I know, but I did think many unkind things about you and my father has always said that if one is in the wrong one must not be ashamed to say so.'

'Your father was right,' Sir Hengist said. 'But your courage is something that I might have expected of his daughter.'

'My courage?' Andora questioned.

'Yes,' he answered. 'It was courageous of you to confess a fault. Come, be honest, it was not easy, was it?'

He reached out unexpectedly and took her hand in his. It was either his touch or his words which made her feel confused.

'It was indeed hard to find words,' she answered. 'But I am sorry for having been unjust.'

'And now that has been put straight,' Sir Hengist said, 'perhaps you will listen to me. I think really the best thing would be for you to go home.'

'Go home!' Andora cried in astonishment. 'Why should you say that?'

'Because I am afraid that you may be

spoiled,' he said. 'Country mice, when they come to town, get dissatisfied with themselves. They want to be like the town mice and they do not realise what a mistake that would be.'

'I do not know about being a mistake,' Andora said in a soft, serious voice. 'It is very hard to be only a simple person amongst all this grandeur and splendour. You saw when I arrived, everything about me is old-fashioned and out-of-date — my coach, my clothes, I think perhaps even the way I think.'

'But that is what makes you so different,' Sir Hengist said quickly.

'So different that it caused you a great deal of amusement,' Andora retorted. 'I thank you, Sir, but I have no desire to be a butt for the laughter of bored gallants.'

His laughter rang out at her words and then, as she turned away from him as if she would leave the garden, he held tightly on to her hand so that she could not escape.

'Oh, Andora! Andora!' he cried. 'You are such a child! And it seems that I must now apologise to you. I did not realise that my laughter had hurt you or that you had been angry with me because of it.'

'No one likes being laughed at,' Andora said hotly.

'Least of all a country mouse,' he added gently. 'Forgive me. It was wrong of me. Nay, more, it was cruel.'

Her face was still turned away from him and now he reached out and took her by the shoulders, turning her round to face him.

'Will you not forgive me?' he asked. And then, as she hesitated, he went down on one knee. 'See, I am petitioning you.'

'I thought in the night,' Andora said slowly, 'that it was foolish and petty of me to mind. But one cannot help one's feelings and I did mind — perhaps because I was alone and frightened.'

'You are making me feel lower than the dust,' Sir Hengist said. His face was serious and his eyes were not laughing at her. 'Are you going to forgive me, Andora?'

'Of course,' she answered, 'so long as you will, in return, forgive me.'

He rose to his feet.

'That is a bargain,' he said and bending his head kissed her hand.

She thought to herself that it was the first time any man's lips had ever touched her skin, and then before she could think more of it he had released her hand and stood towering above her.

'You must go back,' he said, 'or the others will wonder what is keeping you. Meet me here tomorrow. Her Majesty will doubtless give you another note; if not, I will have one for her.'

Andora knew herself dismissed. At the same time she hesitated. Shyly and a little timidly she said:

'Thank you.'

'For what?' Sir Hengist asked in surprise.

'For . . . for being kind to me,' Andora whispered, and then without waiting for an answer she hurried away, half running through the rose garden on to the lawns beyond.

She had a feeling that he was gazing after her, but she did not look back. She only knew that she felt bewildered and surprised by what had happened. But she was conscious at the same time that something dark and lowering which had lain like a load on her heart had been lifted. And as she reached the Palace she realised that it was the hatred that had been festering against Sir Hengist since she had arrived.

She carried the note that Sir Hengist had given her to the Royal Apartments. The Queen was working in the sitting-room which led off her bed chamber, seated at her desk, surrounded by State papers, a white quill in her hand.

Elizabeth looked up impatiently as

Andora curtsied before her.

'Well, what is it?' she said sharply.

'A note, Your Majesty, from my Lord Essex.'

Elizabeth's face cleared. She threw down the quill and put out her hands eagerly.

'Give it to me,' she said with the eagerness of a young girl grasping at her first token of love.

Andora gave the scroll of parchment into her hand. The Queen tore it open and read it with a secret smile on her face. Then she rose to her feet and walked across the room to stand at the window looking out over the river.

Andora watched her, not certain whether she should withdraw without permission or whether by staying she was intruding on the Queen's thoughts. There was silence in the room save for the buzzing of a big bumble-bee around the flowers, which were arranged on a gilt table.

'Have you ever been in love?' the Queen asked unexpectedly.

'No, Your Majesty.'

'Then you're lucky,' Elizabeth said. 'Love is a two-edged weapon, child, for while it brings joy it also brings pain.'

She was silent for a moment and then continued:

'Who would not envy me at this moment? Ruler of this great land, holding the hearts of my subjects, being served as no woman has ever been served before by men of courage and learning. And, yet, however much one has, love always makes one demand more.'

'What more could Your Majesty want?' Andora asked.

The Queen swung round.

'I want youth! Youth!' she replied. 'Do you think I am not aware how quickly the years are passing? Do you think I am so foolish that I do not realise that every month makes it more difficult for me to draw to me those things which matter more to any woman than gold, jewels, power and position?'

She walked restlessly across the room, moving so lightly and with such grace that it seemed to Andora impossible to believe that she was, in fact, much more than a girl. But in the sunlight there were wrinkles beneath her eyes and deep lines at the corners of her mouth.

Then with a bewildering change of mood the Queen said:

'Here I am talking to you as if I were a woman instead of speaking as a Queen. It is the Throne that matters, Andora Bland.

Not you or I individually, but the Throne, which must be built not only on men's lives but on their affection. Remember that. It is something which must never be forgotten.'

Andora's lips parted, but before she could speak the Queen went on briskly:

'And now go, for I have work which must be done.'

Andora curtsied and went from the room, feeling, as she had felt before, that she had been blown about by boisterous winds which had left her breathless.

She hurried down the passages trying to find her way back to her own apartment. She must have taken the wrong turning for she found herself in the audience chamber which was filled with people of all sorts and conditions. The Queen usually granted a time late in the afternoon when petitions might be placed before her.

There was a group of nobles conversing together near the empty Throne, but as Andora passed by them, remembering that there was an exit at the far end of the chamber which led directly to the Maids-of-Honours' apartments above, she saw a gallant wearing a sword turn round hastily and in doing so dig the scabbard into the leg of a man who stood behind him.

'*Caramba!*' the injured gallant exclaimed.

'You careless clod! You have ruined a new pair of silk hose by your clumsiness. I have a good mind to charge you for them.'

'I am desolated,' the man with the sword apologised. 'If I win at cards this evening, I swear I will make you a gift of a dozen pairs.'

'That is an easy promise,' the other man retorted. 'I have never known you to win, not in all the years I have been playing with you.'

There was some laughter at this and none of them noticed Andora slipping past them, but as she reached the door on the other side of the chamber she turned and looked back. The exclamation made by the man who had been struck by the sword had been in the nature of an oath. All the same it had been a strange one. It was only now that she realised what it was and where she had heard it before.

She could see clearly a little boy running across the courtyard holding in his hand a jam tart which had been given him by the cook. One of the dogs had run to meet him and as he swerved to avoid the animal he had slipped and fallen down on the cobbles, covering himself and the jam tart with mud from the recent rains.

'*Caramba!*' he exclaimed.

His mother, who was Andora's Spanish

nurse, had risen from the window where she had been sewing and hurried out to him. Picking him up, for by now he was crying at the loss of his tart, she said:

'Stop your noise, you naughty boy, and do not ever let me hear you say that word again, for I will not have swearing of any sort in this house from you or any other child.'

'But my father says it,' the boy had protested through his tears.

'Men may say a lot of things which it is not good for little boys to repeat,' the nurse had said severely. 'And remember in future you are not to let it pass your lips. Is that understood?'

She wiped him down and brought him back to the house still sobbing a little and sent him through the inner passage back to the kitchen to beg the cook for another tart. Then she rejoined Andora in the nursery.

'Why is *caramba* a bad word?' Andora enquired.

'All oaths are bad,' she replied. 'But *caramba* is a common oath used only by the Spanish people of no import. Noblemen swear in a different way when it pleases them to do so.'

'Tell me what they say,' Andora pleaded.

'Certainly not,' her nurse had replied.

'The Spanish you learn from me will be the Spanish as spoken by the gentry and not by the riff-raff of the towns and villages.'

Caramba! An oath of the Spanish riff-raff. And yet it had been spoken here in the Palace of Greenwich by a man who appeared to be a nobleman.

What was the explanation? Andora asked herself. Had it just been surprised out of him by the sharp point of the sword? She turned to see one of the Ushers standing near her.

'Excuse me,' she said, 'but would you be kind enough to tell me who the gentleman is in the orange doublet wearing a chain set with sapphires? You will see him a little to the right of the Throne.'

'That is Lord Braye,' the Usher replied.

'Who is he?' Andora asked.

The Usher shrugged his shoulders.

'I do not know much about him,' he said.

Andora slipped away and up the stairs to her own bed chamber. Had she, by some strange chance, overheard something which might prove of great import? she wondered. Who was Lord Braye and why should he speak Spanish?

When the Maids-of-Honour had re-assembled about half-an-hour later she asked Margaret Edgecombe, who was quiet

104

and modest and therefore a girl to whom Andora instinctively felt drawn in friendship, if she had ever met Lord Braye.

'I have seen him out riding with Her Majesty,' Margaret answered. 'He seemed to amuse her with what he was saying. Otherwise I know very little about him — but, then, I have not been here long.'

'I must find out more,' Andora thought, and that evening, after they had dined and when the Queen was, as usual, dancing with Lord Essex, she contrived to move around the room until she was standing within a few feet of Lord Braye.

She saw that he was older than she had thought at first — in fact he must be nearly middle-aged — with protruding brown eyes and sensuous thick lips. He was not handsome and yet he was so splendidly dressed that it was impossible not to notice him. There were jewels flashing on the chain he wore round his neck and in his right ear was a magnificent sapphire which matched the one in his ring. His doublet was of white satin embroidered with pearls and he seemed to be flirting rather daringly with the Duchess of Suffolk.

Andora tried to listen to their conversation, but it was all carried on in very low voices so it was impossible for her to hear anything but a few words of compliment and provocative repartee which told her nothing of what she wanted to know.

She wondered whether she should report to Sir Hengist what she had overheard, and then thought that in all probability he would laugh at her and tell her she had been mistaken. After all, an oath was little to go on, and she sensed, although no one seemed disposed to tell her, that Lord Braye was of importance and well trusted at Court.

'I must know more, I must,' Andora thought to herself. She watched him all the evening while he flirted with this lady and then with another. There was nothing in his behaviour that was in any way different from any of the other gallants and noblemen.

The following morning the Queen announced after breakfast that she intended to go riding. She told her Maids-of-Honour that she would not require any of their services and that they could apply themselves instead to their studies and their needlework until her return.

She rode off with a dozen gentlemen into the woods, Lord Essex at her side and Sir Walter Raleigh a little behind, vying for the Queen's favours whenever he had the chance. Andora saw them go with a little sigh of relief.

She had planned this morning that she would write a long letter to her father, telling him of first impressions at Court, but not, of course, entrusting to a letter the secret commission that had been given her by Lord Burleigh and Sir Francis Walsingham. That would have to wait until they met, but she wondered if she could convey in some way to her father that she had been singled out for their favour, because she knew how greatly it would please him.

She had just turned in through the main doorway of the Palace with the other Maids-in-Honour when she saw in front of her an elegant figure in a cloak of salmon pink velvet. She knew even before she saw his face who it was, and as he turned to the left down one of the long galleries overlooking the river, she slipped away from Margaret Edgecombe and Mary Howard and followed him.

He was some way ahead of her and she could hear him humming a little tune as he swung along, passing through the Long Gallery and down a passage which crossed into another wing of the Palace.

Andora crept behind. The passages were deserted at this time of the morning save for a few valets scurrying by with their masters' clothes over their arms or carrying trays of coffee or brandy to those gallants who had not yet risen despite the lateness of the hour.

Lord Braye never looked back. He passed down another passage and then, opening a door, went inside. The door shut behind him and Andora, after waiting a few seconds, walked up to it to see what was written on the card which was pinned above the knocker.

All the apartments in the Palace had the card of the occupant on the outer door. Here, as she had expected, she saw inscribed: *'The Most Honourable Lord Braye'*.

She was just about to turn and walk away again when suddenly the door opened.

'Good morning! You were seeking me?' a voice asked.

She looked up in confusion to see that Lord Braye stood there.

'I . . . I think I have made a mistake,' she said quickly. 'I thought . . .'

'No, indeed, there is no mistake,' he answered, and putting out his hand drew her by the arm in through the doorway.

'No, no,' she insisted. 'I thought that . . . that so . . . someone else lived in this apartment — I . . .' her voice trailed away ineffectually. 'I pray you, Sir, unhand me.'

Forcibly holding her arm so that she could not escape, he drew her through the hall into which they had just entered and through another door into a large room. It was a sitting-room, exquisitely furnished with a splendour and luxury which seemed to echo Lord Braye's apparel. Chairs were heaped with velvet cushions and there was a couch drawn up in front of the fireplace.

Now that they had entered the room Lord Braye released her arm and closed the door behind him.

'You are Andora Bland, are you not?' he asked.

'Yes, indeed,' Andora said. 'But I cannot stay here and, as I told your Lordship, I was looking for . . . for someone and came to the wrong place.'

'You lie,' he answered, 'but very charmingly. You were looking for me.'

'I . . . I do not know . . . why you should s . . . say that,' Andora stammered.

He took off his cloak and flung it down on a chair, and then advanced towards her both arms outstretched.

'Andora, you are entrancing,' he said. 'Quite entrancing. That flawless skin; that fair hair like golden corn; those rosebud lips. How is it that I did not see you first?'

Andora tried to pull her hands away from his.

'My Lord, let me go,' she pleaded. 'It is not seemly that I should be here in your apartment.'

'Who will know?' he asked. 'Besides, have you forgotten? You followed me.'

'I . . .' Andora began, only to be silenced as he laid his fingers against her lips.

'No, no,' he said, 'do not prevaricate. When something happens, such as has happened to you and me, it is stupid to protest over much or, indeed, to deny it. You saw me last night and I know what you felt! But it was not possible for me to pay any attention to you at the time. It would have caused comment and, indeed, jealousy, as I think you can understand. This morning we are alone.'

'I am afraid, my Lord, we are talking at cross purposes,' Andora said quickly.

'Oh, Andora, do not play with me,' Lord Braye replied. 'We may never have this golden opportunity again. Don't let us waste the precious minutes by setting up barriers which can so easily be destroyed by your red lips.'

'My Lord, I must go,' Andora cried.

She turned and ran towards the door but, moving swiftly, he caught her in his arms before she reached it and held her close to him.

'You are shy,' he said triumphantly. 'Shy and a little afraid because I have discovered your secret. Do not be afraid of me, Andora, I will love you, even as you love me. That is all that matters, is it not?'

'I do not love you,' Andora cried, warding him off with her hands as effectively as she could.

'Do not expect me to believe that,' he said fondly. 'You followed me here; have you forgotten? It was clever of you — cleverer than I expected you to be. My dear, I saw your eyes last night when you were watching me and I knew then that Cupid's arrow had found its mark in your heart even as now it has found it in mine.'

'Please . . . please, listen to me,' Andora said. 'This is all a mistake.'

'I am not going to listen to you,' he retorted. 'I only want to tell you that I love you. I love your worried little blue eyes — and most of all I love your mouth.'

He crushed her to him suddenly and in a kind of sick horror she realised that he was about to kiss her. She struggled wildly, but it was too late. His lips, hot and moist and possessive, clung to hers.

She fought and struggled, but to no avail.

For the first time she realised how strong a man could be and how small and ineffective she was in comparison.

'Andora!'

She heard him speak her name hoarsely with an undercurrent of desire that she had never heard in a man's voice before. And then as she gasped for breath she saw his eyes looking down into hers with a fire behind them and a passion that she had never known could so transform any man's face.

'Let . . . me . . . go! Let . . . me . . . go!' she cried wildly. 'There has been . . . a mistake. You do not . . . understand.'

She heard him laugh, but it was more a sound of triumph and of victory than of humour. He swept her up into his arms and while she pushed against him with her hands he carried her bodily across the room towards the couch.

She tried to scream, but as he set her down his mouth was on hers again and after one little cry she was silenced.

'You are adorable, entrancing,' she heard him murmur excitedly and then she felt his weight upon her and the soft white and silver of her gown tore beneath his fingers.

She felt the full horror of it seep over her as if she went down into deep waters and she was being drowned beneath them. She felt a sudden faintness come over her — the faintness of fear, horror and sheer, abject terror.

And then, as his lips seemed to crush all life from her, she heard the door open and a voice, icily cold like a naked rapier, ask:

'Am I intruding, my Lord?'

5

Lord Braye struggled to his feet.

'*Nom de Dieu!*' he ejaculated. 'What the devil do you want?'

Andora felt the mist clear between her eyes and the feeling that she was sinking into a terrifying darkness begin to vanish. But it was still as if he spoke from far, far away that she heard Sir Hengist's voice say sharply:

'I bring a message, my Lord, from the Earl of Essex. He asks if you will play tennis with him this afternoon.'

'Tennis!' Lord Braye exclaimed almost hysterically. 'And for that you burst into my apartments!'

'I must apologise if my presence is unwelcome,' Sir Hengist said. 'When I knocked on the outer door there was no answer and knowing you were here, I felt that you would wish to reply immediately to the invitation which my Lord Essex has extended to you.'

'Yes, yes, of course, and I accept,' Lord

Braye said testily.

Still in a daze, Andora managed to slip off the couch. In a humiliation which was beyond expression she was conscious of her torn gown, her bruised mouth and her untidy hair. She felt so weak that if she had not held on to the back of a chair she might have fallen to the floor.

But more than anything else she was conscious of the scorn and the distaste in Sir Hengist's expression as his eyes flickered over her. She wanted to run to him, to beg his protection, to plead with him to take her away. Instead, she could only stand there trembling, her fingers ineffectually trying to draw the remnants of her bodice across the whiteness of her bosom.

It was then, just as she thought he was about to leave her, to turn and go from the room, that Sir Hengist spoke to her directly.

'Mistress Bland, I think,' he said in a doubtful tone, as if he was finding it difficult to recognise her. 'I heard Mistress Blanche Parry enquiring for you a short while ago. Will you not permit me to escort you to her apartment?'

'Please! Please!' Andora said, the words forced between her lips with the violence of her feelings and yet sounding little more than a whisper.

She had moved towards him, conscious as she did so that Lord Braye put out his hand as if to prevent her and then thought better of it. With what seemed to her an almost superhuman effort she reached Sir Hengist's side.

'Take me . . . away,' she murmured. 'Please . . . take me away.'

He barely glanced at her but bowed to Lord Braye.

'I will inform my Lord Essex,' he said, 'that your Lordship will meet him on the tennis court at six o'clock this evening. He will, I know, be looking forward to the game.'

'I thank you.'

The words were a snarl rather than an expression of politeness.

And then Andora was out of the room into the outer hall and a second later had stepped through the door labelled with Lord Braye's name into the passage outside. Sir Hengist looked to the right and then to the left.

'Come this way,' he said. 'There is a staircase which leads into the gardens. We are less likely to be seen there than in the Long Gallery.'

He strode ahead and meekly she followed him. They reached the staircase, its narrow stone steps leading to a door which opened into the Privy gardens. It was as they came into the sunlight that Andora managed to find her voice.

'I did . . . not know that . . . that he had seen me . . . following him,' she faltered. 'I heard . . . him . . .'

'If you were my daughter,' Sir Hengist interrupted, 'I would have you soundly whipped and sent back to the country. You must be deranged if you think you can go alone into a man's lodgings without losing both your virtue and your reputation.'

'But I did not mean to,' Andora expostulated. 'He dragged me in when he found me outside the door.'

'Yet you say you followed him.'

'Yes, because . . . because I heard him swear — and in Spanish!'

She spoke the last words almost beneath her breath. Then, to her consternation, Sir Hengist laughed — the laugh she had hated him for before; the laughter which was so characteristic of him, rich and untrammelled.

It was only for a moment that his merriment got the better of him. Then, in a voice serious and vehement, he said:

'I said from the very beginning that this whole project was ridiculous and nonsensical. How were you, a newcomer at Court, to know that Lord Braye's fondest boast is that he can swear — and make love — in every European language?'

Andora's fingers went up in dismay to her bruised mouth. 'You mean . . . that everybody knows that he . . . can speak Spanish?'

'Speak Spanish!' Sir Hengist said scornfully. 'He can no more speak Spanish that I can speak Chinese! He knows a few words of the language, just as he can splutter a few endearments in French. Did you not hear him ejaculate *"Nom de Dieu"* when I interrupted you?'

'Yes, I . . . I did,' Andora faltered.

'God's teeth! If spies were all as nit-witted and as easy to catch as Braye they would have been laid by the heels long ago,' Sir Hengist exclaimed.

'I see that I have been . . . very stupid,' Andora said humbly.

'Stupid,' Sir Hengist stormed. 'Have you imagined what your reputation will be if you have been seen in the bachelor wing of the Palace by anyone of consequence?'

'How did you know I was there?' Andora asked.

'Fortunately my servant saw you, and thinking it strange that a Maid-of-Honour should be about at that hour in the morning, he told me that he had seen you enter Lord Braye's apartments.'

The horror of what she had been through seemed to sweep over Andora like a flood tide.

'You came . . . just in time,' she stammered. 'I . . . I did not know that . . . men could be . . . like that. And what was more he . . . he thought that I had been following him because I . . . had fallen in love with . . . him.'

'The sort of thing that conceited nincompoop would believe!' Sir Hengist sneered. 'But, now, listen to me. You are never — do you understand? — never to go alone to any man's rooms, whoever he may be. You are to forget this tomfool scheme of discovering spies and traitors in Her Majesty's entourage. There are not any, I assure you. The whole thing is a figment of Lord Burleigh's imagination.'

He gave a laugh which was more of a snort.

'He is growing old and suspects treachery where there is none and imagines there are Spaniards up every chimney. Leave the enemy to the fighting men and get on with the task of serving the Queen — the only one of which you are capable.'

His words, spoken in the severe, upbraiding tone of a schoolmaster, seemed to destroy Andora's last vestige of pride and self respect. She felt the tears start into her eyes and knew that what she had been through and all her fears were likely to culminate in a tempest of weeping.

'I am . . . sorry, Sir,' she said in a broken voice. 'Please . . . please say no more. I know that I have been both foolish and reckless, but . . . do not berate me any more, for I . . . cannot bear it.'

She raised her eyes, swimming with tears, to his. Her face was very small and white while her red mouth quivered like that of a child who was being punished almost beyond endurance.

Sir Hengist looked down at her and then it seemed to her that the grimness of his expression softened.

'Andora,' he said in a very different tone. 'It is only that . . .'

What he had been about to say was lost, for at that moment a high, gay, affected voice cried:

'Hengist! As I live and breathe! And here I have been searching the whole Palace for you.'

Andora turned her head quickly. Coming through the gardens towards them was the most beautiful woman she had ever seen in her life! She was sparkling with jewels, her full satin skirts were the colour of ripe peaches and her dark hair dressed high on her head glittered with sapphires and diamonds.

She held out two very slim, bejewelled hands to Sir Hengist and raised a crimson, bow-shaped mouth to his, pouting provocatively.

'You are a bad, wicked man!' she declared. 'I arrived late night and expected to find you waiting on me. When you did not come, I could hardly believe that you had deserted such an old friend.'

'Lilian!' Sir Hengist exclaimed. 'I had no idea you were returning to Court.'

'A year of mourning is long enough, I assure you,' she replied. 'If I had stayed in the country any longer I swear I should have died of *ennui*. But now I am back and, oh, the relief and joy of it.'

'It is a joy we all share,' Sir Hengist said, bowing low and raising her finger to his lips.

Over his bent head the newcomer's eyes turned towards Andora and took in every detail of her dishevelled appearance — her cheeks stained with tears, the torn gown which she was vainly trying to conceal by covering it with her hands, the tousled fair curls flowing round her forehead in the summer breeze.

As Sir Hengist straightened himself, he must have seen the two women looking at each other and said hastily:

'Lilian, may I present Mistress Andora Bland? She has been involved in . . . in an accident and I am just escorting her back to Mistress Parry. Andora, this is the Countess of Malvern, without whom the Court has been exceedingly dull for the past year.'

'An accident!' Lady Malvern exclaimed, and it seemed to Andora that the suspicion that had been very obvious in her face cleared. 'Poor child! What happened?'

'Her coach lost a wheel,' Sir Hengist said quickly. 'And as she is somewhat bruised I think it best if we take her immediately to the entrance to the Maids-of-Honours' apartments.'

'Yes, yes, of course,' Lady Malvern said. 'We will all walk that way. It must, indeed, have been a very nasty shock for Mistress Bland!'

She paused and then added in a low voice which was intended only for Sir Hengist's ears:

'I thought for one moment, Hengist, that you had been up to your tricks.'

'How can you be so mistaken in me?' he

asked and she laughed, a gay, musical laugh which seemed to hang on the air like the chime of little bells.

'Tell me all that has been happening,' she said. 'If you only knew what it has been like sitting in a house with drawn blinds, wearing that hideous black, which never did become me, and listening to the moans and groans of my mother-in-law — a more deadly and boring woman never existed.'

'But now you have escaped,' Sir Hengist smiled.

They were all three walking across the green lawn which led to the other side of the Palace. If Andora had dared, she would have run ahead. As it was, she could only move miserably at Sir Hengist's side wishing the earth would swallow her up, wishing almost that she were dead rather than that he, or anyone else, should compare her with the lovely lady at his other side.

'So you are in attendance on Lord Essex,' Lady Malvern was saying. 'What a precarious post, *mon brave* — but entertaining so long as it lasts.'

'He is utterly devoted to Her Majesty,' Sir Hengist said.

'And she to him, by all accounts,' Lady Malvern said lightly. 'But he is not the first,

123

although, indeed, he may be the last. What news of Leicester?'

'He is in the Low Countries.'

'And that is where he had better stay,' Lady Malvern laughed. 'I hear the Queen is furious with him over the amount of money he has been spending and the fact that his wife has a Court which rivals in splendour not only Greenwich but Whitehall and Hampton Court combined.'

'I see you have learnt all the gossip in the last twenty-four hours,' Sir Hengist said.

'I have not heard all that I wanted to hear,' Lady Malvern replied. 'For you know, Hengist, what I am really interested in is — you.'

Her voice softened on the pronoun. Out of the corner of her eye Andora saw Lady Malvern lay her hand on Sir Hengist's arm in a gesture both affectionate and intimate.

By this time they were within a few yards of the door that she recognised as leading to the Queen's apartments. Swiftly she turned and dropped a curtsy first to Lady Malvern and then to Sir Hengist.

'Thank you,' she said. 'I can find my way now.'

It was only as she spoke that quite unaccountably the tears welled once again into her eyes and her voice faltered. To her own dismay she heard a sob which seemed to rend her body and come from her very heart.

'Wait! Andora! Wait!' she heard Sir Hengist say; but already she had turned and run through the open doorway and up the stairs, feeling her way blindly, for it was impossible to see as she was shaken by the storm of tears which would no longer be denied.

How she reached her own room she did not know. Fortunately she met no one on the way and slamming the door behind her she flung herself on to her bed and buried her face in her pillow. She cried as she had not cried since she was a child, with an abandon which was utterly desolate . . .

It seemed to her as if the whole world was dark and empty. The terror of Lord Braye's attack; the humiliation of the scorn and contempt in Sir Hengist's voice; the manner in which he had told her how foolish she was. All this she thought she could have borne if she had not, in her stupidity, shattered and destroyed the friendship which she had felt he had offered her after they had talked together in the rose garden.

She had not known it until now, but from that moment she had begun to trust him. Now he despised her and, what was more, she told herself miserably, it was not likely that he would think of her again now that his friend had returned to Court — the spectacularly beautiful Countess of Malvern.

Wearily, after a long time, Andora dragged herself from the bed and rang the bell for her maid, Grace. However miserable she felt, if she was to be ready by the time the Queen returned, something must be done about her gown.

Grace came hurrying at the summons, entered the room and exclaimed with horror at Andora's appearance.

'Whatever have you been adoing to yourself, Mistress?' she enquired. 'You look as if you had been set upon by Highwaymen or Cut-throats.'

'I think that is exactly what has happened to me,' Andora said miserably. 'Will you mend my gown, Grace?'

'That can be mended,' Grace answered, 'but we must also see to your face and to your hair. Is it for some man for whom you're acrying?'

It was an impertinent question, but Andora knew full well that Grace did not mean to be impertinent. She was just a country girl who spoke her mind.

'It is not one man who has upset me but two,' Andora answered. 'And, oh, Grace!

You were right. This place is full of evil. I did not understand before what men were like.'

'I warned you, Mistress,' Grace said. 'They're all the same. 'Tis hard, indeed, for a woman to keep herself pure and virtuous in the Queen's Palace, for all that Her Majesty has contrived to be a virgin for over fifty years.'

Andora took off her gown and Grace poured cold water into a basin so that she could bathe her face.

'There are scratches on your shoulders, Mistress,' Grace pointed out.

'I know. They will heal,' Andora said, 'but I do not think I shall ever be able to trust a man again.'

Before Grace could reply, there came a knock at the door. The girl went to open it. There was a murmured conversation before she returned with a bouquet of flowers and a note.

'From my Lord Murton,' she said.

'Give them back,' Andora said a little wildly. 'I do not want them. I do not want flowers from anyone.'

Grace had already shut the door. Now she put the flowers down on the table.

' 'Tis not his Lordship who has been upsetting you, Mistress,' she said shrewdly.

Andora, splashing the cold water against her eyes, shook her head.

'I thought not,' Grace said. 'The more I hear of his Lordship the more I am sure he's a decent gentleman and one whose word a lady can trust. Rich too! 'Twill be a fine marriage for anyone who becomes his wife.'

Andora turned round to face her.

'Grace, you are not matchmaking, are you?'

'And why not?' Grace asked defiantly. 'A woman is best married when she's young. Those who stay too long in the Palace get corrupted — or else they fall in love with people as is not for them.'

'What do you mean by that?' Andora asked curiously.

'Well, there's Lady Mary Howard,' Grace said. 'Her maid tells me she's that besotted with m'Lord Essex that she cries out his name in her sleep. If the Queen hears of it, she'll suffer for her love as so many have before her.'

Andora looked frightened. She, too, had heard the stories of Maids-of-Honour who had loved noblemen of whom the Queen did not approve and who had been either sent to the Tower or otherwise severely punished for their presumption.

'Then there's Lady Elizabeth Throckmorton,' Grace went on. 'It is well known that she is casting her eyes in the direction of Sir Walter Raleigh.'

'Oh, no! That cannot be!' Andora exclaimed.

'That is what they say,' Grace replied. 'And the Queen will not be pleased about that either, for she looks on Sir Walter as her most devoted admirer.'

'I only hope what you tell me is not true,' Andora said, seating herself at the dressing-table to rearrange her hair.

'That is why 'twould be best for you to be married soon, Mistress,' Grace said. 'Before Her Majesty looks on you as indispensible. Once the Queen grows really fond of a Maid-of-Honour she will put every obstacle in the way should she wish to get married.'

'You speak as if I had the offer,' Andora answered. 'Why, I barely know Lord Murton, and I suspect that the pretty things he says to me he also says to a dozen other ladies.'

'They speak well of him below stairs,' Grace said insistently. 'Read his note, Mistress, and see what he has to say.'

She brought the note and put it down in front of Andora. Andora picked it up but somehow felt reluctant to unroll it.

'I hate all men,' she said aloud, remembering that fire in Lord Braye's eyes and the feeling of his thick, passionate lips.

'Maybe,' Grace said, 'but no woman can live without a man; and all women, whether they be noble or lowly, require a husband.'

Andora laughed a little shakily.

'You are so full of good commonsense, Grace,' she said, 'that almost you persuade me against my own inclination.'

She looked down at the note. There were only a few lines.

I pray that you think of me sometimes, for I can think of nothing but you.
                                                    Murton

Andora threw the note down on the dressing-table and rose to her feet. Only a few days ago she had been in the country with none of these problems and difficulties. She had been free and untrammelled, content to walk by the stream as it bubbled over the stones or to sit beside the water-lily pond watching the fish eat the May-flies as they settled upon the water. It had all been so calm and peaceful, so different from the tumult and chaos which seemed to surround her now.

The door was opened suddenly and Mistress Blanche Parry stood there.

'It is rumoured that you have had an accident, child,' she said.

'It is nothing, Ma'am,' Andora replied.

'But my Lady Malvern tells me that she met you with Sir Hengist and that your gown was torn and you were in tears. What occurred?'

'I . . . I assure you it was . . . of little importance,' Andora answered. 'I got . . . knocked down by one of the carriages approaching the Palace.'

The lie came hesitantly from between her lips and she knew that she was blushing. Ever since she was a child she had found it extremely difficult to tell a falsehood convincingly.

'I have spoken to the Queen before about the narrowness of the courtyard,' Mistress Parry said almost triumphantly. 'The coaches come in too fast and the coachmen have not got proper control of their horses. Well, we shall be moving to Hampton Court next month, and a good thing, too. There is not enough room in this place for half the people who try to squeeze in on us.'

She looked across the room to where Grace was sewing the white and silver gown.

'There is another gown ready for your

mistress. The seamstress finished it a few hours ago. Let her wear that.'

Grace rose to her feet.

'I will go and fetch it, Mistress,' she said respectfully, dropping a small curtsy.

When she had gone from the room, Mistress Parry closed the door behind her.

'Lady Malvern said you were with Sir Hengist,' she said to Andora.

'Yes, Sir Hengist found me,' Andora replied.

'As you are new here from the country, I think I should give you a word of warning,' Mistress Parry said severely. 'Keep away from Sir Hengist.'

Andora's eyes widened.

'What's wrong with him?' she asked.

'There is nothing wrong,' Mistress Parry said tartly. 'But these buccaneers are all the same — Sir Francis Drake, Sir Hengist Wake, Jack Hawkins, Sir Walter Raleigh. I would not trust any of them on a dark night farther than I could see them. You are too young, Andora, to get mixed up with men of that sort.'

'I do not think Sir Hengist is in the least interested in me,' Andora said, feeling it was only fair that she should make that clear.

'One never knows,' Mistress Parry said darkly. 'You are a pretty girl and a new face

132

about the Court. I have always found these two things make an almost irresistible appeal to the swashbucklers.'

She glanced towards the flowers on the table.

'Another bouquet from Lord Murton?' she enquired.

Andora reflected that Mistress Parry knew everything. She had been with the Queen so long and was so intimate with all the Maids-of-Honour that nothing, however trivial, escaped her notice.

'I think his Lordship makes a habit of sending bouquets to strangers,' Andora said.

'He has not done so to many women before,' Mistress Parry said. 'Not like Sir Hengist, for instance.'

'Is Sir Hengist interested in the Countess of Malvern?' Andora asked.

She did not know why, but the question seemed a significant one. Mistress Parry paused before she answered.

'My Lady Malvern was married when she was very young to an old man,' she said. 'Undoubtedly she had a difficult time in attuning her youth and high spirits to the slower pace of her Lord and master. Now his Lordship has passed to his Maker and my Lady Malvern has been able to return to us.'

'You have not answered my question,' Andora insisted.

'About Sir Hengist?' Mistress Parry queried. 'Well, I should not be surprised to see a real romance take place between those two! In a way they would be well suited to each other. Lilian Malvern would keep Sir Hengist in order, but he would be very fortunate if she condescended to bestow her hand upon him. There are many noblemen at Court who would give their right hand for a smile from Lady Malvern — and a great deal more if they got the chance of marrying her.'

'She is very beautiful,' Andora said in a flat voice.

'Beautiful, amusing and very intelligent — all in one person,' Mistress Parry said triumphantly. 'Sounds like one of my fortunes come true, does it not? That reminds me, Andora, I must tell your fortune with the cards. The girls always plague me to do the newcomers. They say it is more exciting when I know very little about the person I am telling.'

'I do not think you would find my future very exciting,' Andora said with a sigh.

'Do not sound so despondent,' Mistress Parry laughed. 'There may be something exciting for you round the next corner; who knows?'

134

She gave a little laugh and walked towards the door.

'What about Lord Murton?' she said roguishly as she lifted the latch.

Andora did not reply and Mistress Parry went out of the door, closing it quietly behind her.

Andora picked up the bouquet of roses. She smelt the fragrance of them and then suddenly dashed them on to the floor.

'A curse on Lord Murton!' she cried. 'Curse all men! I hate them! I hate them all!'

Once again the tears were streaming down her face.

6

Lady Malvern tried a necklace of rubies round her white neck, then threw it petulantly down on the dressing-table.

'Rubies do not look well with my new gown,' she said to her maid. 'Bring me the pearls.'

She spoke sharply in an arrogant tone which those of her household knew only too well.

The maid brought her a rope of pearls and Lady Malvern wound them around her neck.

'You can leave me now,' she said. 'Tell the flunkeys to let me know when Master Kirk arrives.'

'Very good, m'Lady.'

The maid curtsied and withdrew. Lilian Malvern sat staring at her face in the mirror. For a few minutes she arranged a curl here and there, touched her cheeks with a rabbit's foot and added a little salve to her lips. Then she stared with unseeing eyes, looking not at her own beautiful face but into the future.

She had been a fool, she thought, to let Julian Kirk come to the Palace once she had moved in. He had served to pass the time in the country and it was not her fault if he had become so besotted with her that he had threatened to kill himself if she would not see him. He was a stupid young man of no consequence and she had no intention of ruining her reputation by getting herself talked about with him in London as she had done in the country.

She could hear her mother-in-law's voice still echoing in her ears.

'You are nothing but a strumpet!' the old lady had stormed. 'You drove my son to his death by your infidelities and your heartlessness. Go back to the city gutters where you belong. There is no place for you in the decent, clean countryside.'

Lilian Malvern had laughed at the old woman insolently. She had known that the Dowager had no power to hurt her, for her accusations would not be supported by anyone else. Indeed, they would be refuted by everyone in the neighbourhood save the servants in the Castle and then only those of them who were in close attendance upon her.

She was too clever not to placate the burly

country squires and their dowdy, boring wives. She was always charming to them when she met them and she would speak in a soft, sweet voice of her ailing husband and his elderly mother, saying how happy she was that she could try to nurse them into better health. Some people might find life at the Castle was quiet, she would say with a smile, but she found the hours of the day passed quickly because she was so busy nursing and tending the invalids.

Only her personal maid knew that she lay abed in the morning and as often as not refused to go to her husband when he sent for her.

'His Lordship requires your presence, m'Lady.'

'Tell His Lordship I am asleep.'

'His Lordship knows that is untrue. He asked an hour ago if you had rung for your chocolate.'

'Well, tell him I have a headache or have gone out — anything you like, but do not worry me with his incessant requests,' Lady Malvern would snap.

The maid would turn away with pursed lips to do her bidding.

A year of a querulous husband who would not die. A year of mourning alone with that ghastly old harridan who was her mother-in-law. Was any woman in her full beauty so bedevilled? Lilian asked herself not once but a thousand times. And it might have been longer still but for certain things — a dose of laudanum given instead of the physician's medicine . . . a pillow held close over a sleeping man. . . .

Lilian Malvern gave herself a shake and jumped up from the dressing-table. She had sworn she would never think of that. It was a secret to lie hidden in her own breast for all time. There was no point in dwelling on it. It was over and done with. Now a new life opened before her.

She walked across to the window and took a deep breath of air. Thank God it was not fragrant with the scent of the flowers and the freshness of newcut hay. Instead there was the exciting, dusty, dirty smell of London mixed with the odour of the Palace — ancient, damp and somehow musty. How well she knew them both — how much she loved them!

She moved from the window to walk backwards and forwards across the polished boards. She would get rid of Julian Kirk. He belonged to the past and she did not want ever again to see his adoring eyes, like those of a faithful spaniel, and the young sensitive lips which would tremble when she was cruel.

She admitted it had been exciting, when she had nothing else to do, to slip out at night and meet him in the dark wood where their two estates joined. It had been fun to let down a rope ladder so that he could climb in at her window when all the house was asleep. It had been amusing to drive over to his home and say to that stuck-up mother of his:

'How good-looking and charming your son is! He has grown so tremendously lately that I swear I hardly recognised him.'

How Lady Kirk had hated her because without actually knowing anything definite she had sensed what was going on.

Lilian Malvern smiled at herself in one of the long mirrors which hung between the windows. Well, Lady Kirk could have her son back again. She could send him to Cambridge as she had planned and Julian need make no more objections and prevarications. Home would not seem so attractive when his next-door neighbour was away.

Now for the future.

Lilian Malvern sat down at her dressing-table again and scrutinised her face. She was thirty-two — although she never admitted to anyone, not even to her maid, that she was over twenty-five. Yet time was no respecter of a woman's reticences. There were, at the corner of her eyes, some tiny, faint lines that she had sworn had not been there last year. If she was not mistaken, the line of her chin was not quite as firm as it had been when she left Court in 1585.

'Oh, God! Do not let time go so quickly.'

She uttered the prayer more as an oath than as a petition to the Almighty. She did not really believe in prayer and it was two years since she had been to a religious service.

That was another thing that she had made a mental note that she must remember to do now that she had returned to Court. The Queen expected everyone to attend the services at which she herself put in an appearance. Besides, as Lilian Malvern remembered, Sundays were a great occasion for showing off one's new gowns.

There was only one consolation in having spent so long in the country. She had saved enough money to purchase herself a veritable trousseau of new and fashionable clothes. But they would not last for ever.

'I have got to marry soon.'

She said the words aloud and almost instinctively her fingers went up to touch the tiny lines at the corners of her eyes.

There had been enough gentlemen in attendance on her before she had been forced to retire to the country. But she was a woman of the world and knew that men who sighed and bewailed the fact that she was married might not be so persistent in their intentions now that she was free and they could, if they wished, offer her both their name and their protection.

She ran through the names of those most likely to be interested in her now that she had returned. There were not many and some, regrettably, had already married while she was away. But all the time she was merely playing with the truth because there was no choice as far as she was concerned. She had already made up her mind whom she wanted. She had already decided who was to be her future husband.

She had been in love with him, she thought, since that first day when he had come swashbuckling into the audience chamber behind Sir Francis Drake. The Queen had been in a very gracious mood. She had thanked Sir Francis — which was not surprising considering that the spoils from his last voyage had been astronomical.

'We are very mindful, Sir Francis,' she had said, 'of the value of your cargo and what is more, of the prestige you have brought to this country and the manner in which you have routed the enemy and upheld the dignity of England wherever you have been.'

'Anything I have been able to do,' Sir Francis answered, 'was on behalf of Your Majesty and through the inspiration you gave personally to me and my men before we sailed. We all fought together, not as individuals but as one man who carried against his heart a love knot. That love knot was Your Majesty's smile when you bade us God speed.'

The Queen was pleased and held out her hand for Sir Francis to kiss. As he rose he asked:

'May I present to Your Majesty Master Hengist Wake, who accompanied me on this voyage and has been not only an inestimable help but a very fiery and vigorous champion of England's cause?'

The Queen turned to the big, fair man standing behind Sir Francis.

'I have heard of your prowess, Master Wake,' she said. 'In fact, Lord Burleigh has already related to me many of your exploits and your adventures. We have decided, therefore, that such loyalty and such courage shall not go unrewarded.'

The gentleman-at-arms had brought her the sword. Hengist Wake had knelt before her and she had touched him on each shoulder.

'Arise, Sir Hengist Wake!'

It was the first time Lilian Malvern had seen a man knighted, but she had been more interested in the recipient of the honour than in the ceremony itself.

It had been easy to have Sir Hengist introduced. It had been easy, too, to find out all about him. That he came from an old and noble Somerset family — his father a distant cousin of the Duke of Devon, his mother descended from the Northumberlands. There was blue blood in Sir Hengist Wake's veins, but he seldom spoke of it, preferring to be an individualist and accepted at his own face value.

'Who cares for precedence and all the tiresome trappings of Court?' he had said once when Lilian Malvern had chided him because some popinjay who had recently arrived at Whitehall had taken precedence over him on a ceremonial occasion.

'I care,' she stormed. 'I want you to be important. Do you not understand I only like successful people? I have no use for failures.'

He laughed at her.

'The day I am a failure I will settle in some nice little island in the West Indies and spend the rest of my life listening to the songs of the native girls. They are quite enchanting, by the way.'

'You will come back,' she said confidently, sure of her power over him.

She sighed now to think how certain she had been that he loved her completely and absolutely. But when she retired to the country he had not written to her nor made any attempt to see her.

She had written to him, long, unhappy letters, telling him how boring her life was and how miserable she was to be away from him and from the Court. But although once he sent her a present by an old friend who was visiting in Wiltshire, there had been no personal note, only a formal message hoping that she was in good health and that her husband was convalescing.

'Hengist Wake!'

She said his name aloud and felt her breath come a little quicker. She wondered how often she had whispered that same name as she had gone to sleep at night, sometimes with her eyes wet with tears because she had screamed and raged in one of her tempers until the tears had flown in sheer exasperation.

'I love him!' she told her reflection. 'I have always loved him. There has never really been anyone else but Hengist.'

She was wise enough to know that men

hate to be tied. Once, in the first flush of their passion for each other, he had said to her:

'I shall never marry anyone. The one person I might have married is already tied, and a bachelor fights better because he knows that he is not going to leave a widow and a family behind him.'

She thought how with annoyance that it was the only time he had mentioned marriage. But she would make him propose. It would not be as difficult as all that. Better men than Hengist Wake had lost their heads and their freedom when a beautiful woman had smiled at them and offered them her favours.

'I must not be in a hurry,' Lilian told herself. 'I must let things take their own course. If he thinks I want him, he will run away from me. He likes to be the hunter — he always has. I must play my cards cleverly.'

She shut her eyes for a moment and a sudden tremor ran through her.

'Hengist! Hengist!' she whispered. 'I cannot wait too long.'

She opened her eyes and gave a cynical little laugh at her own emotion. It was not only her body which could not wait for Hengist Wake, it was her purse.

There was a sudden knock on the door.

'Who is it?' Lilian Malvern enquired.

'Master Julian Kirk is here, m'Lady.'

'Tell him I will be with him in a moment,' she replied.

She rose from the dressing-table, conscious that in her new gown, with the pearls around her long neck and her dark hair dressed in the very latest fashion, she looked almost breathtakingly beautiful. She might be going to dismiss her infatuated suitor; but there was no reason why he should not leave her with a picture of all that he was losing vividly and indelibly fixed in his mind.

She picked up her handkerchief from the dressing-table and thought how lovely her long fingers looked against the delicate lawn and lace. There was no doubt about it that, as so many men had told her, every inch of her body was beautiful.

'I must get my portrait painted when I am married,' Lilian thought. 'Hengist can afford the best artist in the country.'

She gave a little sigh of satisfaction. It was nice to think that the man she had decided to marry was not only very attractive but very rich as well.

In another part of the Palace someone else was thinking of Hengist Wake. The Queen, seated at the desk in her private apartments, had just finished writing a note.

'Where is my country mouse?' she asked the assembled Maids-of-Honour. 'I wish this taken to Lord Essex at once.'

'Andora is in the ante-room, Your Majesty,' Mary Radcliffe answered.

'Go and fetch her then,' the Queen commanded.

'Cannot I take it for Your Majesty?' Mary Howard asked.

The Queen shook her head.

'No, my country mouse is a very good messenger. She does not linger by the way and my notes reach their destination with all possible despatch. Besides, I have decided that we shall have some music and I want Lady Mary and Elizabeth Trentham to try their duet together.'

The Maids-of-Honour looked apprehensive. When the Queen made up her mind to listen to their singing or to watch their dancing, she was extremely critical and their performances, more often than not, ended in their being soundly abused and told they must have extra lessons immediately.

Andora, who had been fetched from the ante-room, came hurrying to Her Majesty's side.

'You have a duty for me, Your Majesty?' she enquired.

'Yes, my child,' the Queen replied. 'Take this to Sir Hengist, as you have done before, and then hurry back with anything that he has to give you.'

'Yes, Your Majesty,' Andora said. At the same time her heart dropped. The last person she wished to see at the moment was Sir Hengist and she had hoped that as the Queen had been a little later than usual in repairing to her writing-desk, she would not have to take a note.

There was, however, no possible chance of her protesting or doing anything but what she was told. She only wondered how she could, in fact, face Sir Hengist after what had happened yesterday. She could still hear the scorn in his voice, still see the expression of anger and what she thought was disgust upon his face.

It was not surprising, she thought. If he had only known how she had scrubbed her lips because Lord Braye had kissed them; how she had washed with cold water her shoulders and neck and every other part of her skin that he had touched, and yet felt she would never be able to wash away the memory of what had happened entirely through her own foolishness.

Last night, in despair, she had almost thought that she would run away. How easy to order her coach, to say that she had received bad news from home and must return immediately. Then she had known that because her father was a soldier, because he trusted her, she could not desert her post.

What would he say if he knew that she was in trouble entirely through her own stupidity? How often had he warned her about the intrigues and the gossip of the Court? Of the way a woman's reputation could vanish overnight and a man find himself disgraced simply through not drawing his sword as quickly as was required of him.

Somehow those long discourses her father had given her when he talked of the old days had not seemed connected with herself. They had never appeared to be about real people, and yet now she knew that she could have benefited from his wisdom and his experience had she been a little more attentive.

She went from the Queen's presence into the ante-room and she stopped for a moment to tell Mistress Parry where she was going.

'Do not be long, Andora,' Mistress Parry admonished.

'I shall not, Madam,' Andora replied, and passing through the open door stepped into the passage.

She had not moved more than a few feet down the corridor when she heard a whisper behind her.

'Andora!'

She turned her head. Mary Howard had followed her and was standing just outside the door of the ante-chamber.

'What is it?' Andora asked, retracing her steps.

'Take this note with you,' Mary said, thrusting a small scroll into her hand. 'Give it to Sir Hengist with the one of Her Majesty's and say they are both for my Lord Essex.'

'But, Mary, I cannot do that,' Andora said in a low voice for fear they should be overheard.

'You must. I will tell you about it later. I thought the Queen might send me today and then it would have been easy. Do as I say; tell Sir Hengist they are both for Lord Essex.'

'And what is all this whispering?'

A voice behind them made both girls start violently. The Queen had opened the door while they were talking and they had not heard her. Now she stood there, resplendent in her gown of green shot silk embroidered with gold thread and ornamented with crystal.

'What were you saying?' she repeated.

There was no answer. Elizabeth stepped forward and with her long, ring-laden fingers took from Andora the two notes she held in a hand which seemed to be frozen into immobility.

'As I suspected,' she exclaimed. 'Lady Mary was sending a note to someone. And who could that be?'

The Queen's question was terrifying. Lady Mary went crimson as Elizabeth, tearing open the note which she had given to Andora, read aloud:

'I desire to see you, for there is much I have to say. If you will meet me by the lily pond this evening at five o'clock I can contrive to be there. Please come, for I have not slept because of my longing to see you.

Mary'

The Queen spoke the words in a hard, metallic voice which made every word sound as if it were a pointed weapon to be twisted in the heart of those who listened. Then in a tone of thunder she said:

'To whom is this addressed? Tell me, wench, or I swear I will extort it from you by means of the rack if necessary.'

The colour which had stained Lady Mary's cheeks had now vanished; she was ashen white and trembling so violently that she could scarcely stand. Andora was not surprised. The Queen's anger was terrifying and the flashing light in her eyes would have made a stouter heart quail before her.

Swiftly through Andora's mind flashed all the stories she had ever heard of what happened when the Queen was offended with one of her ladies. The Tower! Exile! Ostracism! But even so they had not committed the madness of casting their eyes at the man whom the Queen herself favoured.

And then Andora remembered how kind Mary Howard had been to her since the first moment she arrived at the Palace. The way she had lent her a gown; her friendliness; the desire that she should not feel left out of all the gossip and the chatter amongst the other Maids-of-Honour.

Impulsively, before Mary could speak, she said:

'May I explain, Your Majesty?'

'As Lady Mary seems tongue-tied — and it is not surprising,' the Queen said icily, 'you may, if you have an explanation, Mistress Bland, offer it to me.'

Andora took a deep breath.

'Lady Mary fancies herself in love, Your

153

Majesty. We have told her it is absurd; but she burns for someone who has not given her any encouragement nor, indeed, I think, ever has even looked her way.'

'And what is the name of this gentleman on whom she has set her affection?' the Queen enquired.

Andora swallowed.

'It is . . . Sir . . . Sir Hengist Wake, Your Majesty.'

'Sir Hengist!'

She heard the surprise in the Queen's voice and saw the frown that had been knitting her brows together ease a little.

'But Sir Hengist has never taken any notice of my ladies,' the Queen said.

'I know, Your Majesty,' Andora answered. 'That is why it is so ridiculous of Lady Mary. We have all told her so; but I think, if the truth be known, it is just a bit of devilment on her part to try and capture his attention because he will look at none of us.'

'So that is it,' the Queen said in a very different tone to Mary Howard. 'At the same time, he must have given you some encouragement for you to write a letter like that.'

Still Lady Mary did not answer. For fear of what she should say Andora interposed quickly:

'I think, Your Majesty, that many women

fall more in love with a man who ignores them than with a man who seeks them out. It is just being contrary — that is what my mother used to say.'

'Sir Hengist! You are sure this note is for Sir Hengist?'

The Queen's eyes seemed to bore into Andora's as if she would drag the very truth from her soul.

'Y. . . yes, Your Majesty. That is whom Lady Mary asked me to give it to and, in fact, I know that is whom she has set her heart on for the moment — though, doubtless, in a week or so it may be someone else.'

'I have said before that I will not have my Maids-of-Honour intriguing with men or having love affairs of any sort,' the Queen said sharply; but now her tone held none of the white fury which had lain behind her words but a little while before.

'You will go to your bedchamber, Lady Mary, and await my decision as to what I shall do about you,' she commanded. 'I am very displeased, very, that you should demean yourself in such a manner or, indeed, run after a gentleman in such a brazen fashion. In future you will behave more circumspectly.'

She looked at the note again, then tore it

into small pieces and threw it onto the floor.

'Pick those up,' she said, 'and do not let me see you again this evening. And, Mistress Bland, kindly remember that you are my messenger, not anyone else's. You, too, will be punished if you carry notes making clandestine appointments. Such things will not be tolerated amongst those who have the honour of waiting upon me.'

'I am sorry, Your Majesty.'

Andora curtsied and the Queen, with one last disapproving glance at Lady Mary, went back to her own apartments. As they heard the door close behind her, Mary raised her eyes and looked at Andora. The full horror of what had occurred swept over both the girls.

'Thank you! Thank you!' Lady Mary said in a voice that seemed almost strangled in her throat; and then without waiting for more Andora fled down the passage.

She hurried across the lawn and reached the rose garden to find Sir Hengist pacing up and down, a scowl between his eyes. She had been so bemused and horrified by what had happened that it was only when she reached his side that she remembered her own troubles and the fact that she had been afraid to encounter him.

'You are very late,' he said accusingly. 'I

cannot stay here all the afternoon cooling my heels.'

'I am sorry,' Andora said. 'Her Majesty was delayed in writing her note and then . . . then something happened.'

She stopped and swallowed convulsively. She realised that she had to tell Sir Hengist what had occurred and for the first time wondered what he would think about the situation in which she had involved him.

'Well, what?' he asked.

There was something uncompromising about the way he looked at her, something which made her feel young, shy and hopelessly inexperienced to deal with this and any of the other situations in which she had been involved since she came to Court.

As if he realised her agitation he added in a kinder tone:

'What is troubling you? Come and sit down for a moment in the arbour. Has Braye been worrying you again?'

'No, no, I have not seen him,' Andora said. 'It is nothing to do with him.'

'Then what is it?' Sir Hengist asked.

They reached the arbour. Andora seated herself, her hands clasped together.

'You are trembling,' he said. 'Do not tell me the Queen has discovered what happened?'

'No, it is nothing to do with me. Well . . . not exactly,' Andora replied, 'although I . . . I am concerned . . .'

Her voice stammered itself into incoherence. Sir Hengist put out his hand and laid it on her trembling fingers.

'Take things slowly,' he said in a kindly tone she had never heard before. 'There is no need to be frightened, Andora. Whatever is upsetting you we can face together, can we not?'

'I hope so,' she answered miserably.

The warmth and strength of his hand was comforting, as was the sound of his voice. She knew, however, that he was likely to take a very different attitude once he had heard what she had done.

'I must tell you quickly,' she said in a low voice. 'The Queen said I was to hurry and not to linger.'

'Go on,' he prompted.

'Lady Mary Howard gave me a note in the corridor outside the Queen's apartments,' Andora said. 'She asked me to give it to you and then, just as I was taking it, the Queen appeared and read it.'

'A note for me!' Sir Hengist exclaimed.

'No, it was not for you,' Andora replied. 'It was for someone else.'

'Lord Essex?' Sir Hengist asked.

Andora nodded.

'The girl must be an idiot!' Sir Hengist ejaculated. 'What did Her Majesty say?'

'She was very angry,' Andora answered. 'The note was not addressed, and having read it aloud Her Majesty asked for whom it was intended.'

'I should have thought that was obvious,' Sir Hengist said. 'But whom did Lady Mary say?'

'She did not say,' Andora answered. 'I think she was too frightened.'

'So what happened?' Sir Hengist enquired.

'I . . . I told the Queen that Lady Mary had given me the note for . . . you, which was the truth,' Andora said.

'Yes, what then?'

'I . . . I said she was . . . in love with you.'

'With me?' Sir Hengist queried in astonishment.

'I had to save her. You do not understand. I had to,' Andora cried desperately.

'So you told Her Majesty that the lady in question was writing love letters to me because she fancied me,' Sir Hengist said.

'I am sorry, terribly sorry,' Andora answered. 'But what else could I do?'

She dropped her head as she spoke, afraid to meet his eyes, waiting for the storm to break over her. And then to her astonishment Sir Hengist laughed — the laugh for which she had hated him a laugh clear and untrammelled which rang out round the empty garden.

'Andora, you little devil!' he chuckled. 'Was there ever such a tangle? Yet I grant you it was the only thing to do.'

She raised her head in astonishment.

'You are not angry with me?'

'Furious,' he answered, but his lips were smiling. 'But I agree with you, to tell the real truth would have been utterly and completely disastrous.'

'I thought you would be en . . . enraged with m . . . me,' Andora stammered.

'I am much more enraged with that little idiot, Mary Howard,' Sir Hengist retorted. 'I have seen her making moon's eyes at Lord Essex and you can tell her from me that he is not the least interested in her.'

'I suppose she cannot help loving him,' Andora said.

'Love! That is not love!' Sir Hengist cried. 'All these yearnings and posturings, all these heart-throbs and languishings. They are not love, child, as you should know. Love is something strong and virile; and when it happens between two people, it is so ecstatic and so magnificent that it cannot be denied.'

Andora looked at him in surprise. She had never expected to hear him speak like this.

'At the same time,' he continued, 'Mary Howard had best look to her behaviour and make her apologies to the Queen in all humbleness.'

'And what will you do?' Andora asked.

'Me?' Sir Hengist enquired. 'I shall do precisely nothing. I cannot help it, can I, if the heart of a foolish girl beats faster?'

He was laughing again and somehow it was so infectious that Andora found herself laughing too. Then suddenly they both stopped.

'If Her Majesty knew the truth!' Andora said apprehensively.

'We would all be for the Tower or the block,' Sir Hengist answered grimly. 'I told you there were dangers here, little Andora, that you did not fully realise.'

'I see there are,' Andora said, rising to her feet. As she did so she had a curious reluctance to release herself from the strength and warmth of his hand, but she was free and she stood looking up at him in the sunshine.

'Thank you! Thank you for being so kind and understanding,' she whispered, and before he could reply she had hurried away, and it was only as she reached the Palace door that she realised that in her anxiety and apprehension over Mary Howard she had forgotten her own embarrassment at meeting Sir Hengist again.

And only the night before she had vowed that she loathed and detested him!

7

It was very hot in the Queen's rooms and the bees buzzing against the window panes seemed to have a somnolent effect on the Maids-of-Honour.

Andora could see that Elizabeth Throckmorton was nodding over her embroidery, and the voice of Margaret Edgecombe, who was reading aloud, seemed to get slower and slower. Even the Queen was relaxed and at ease this afternoon and when Margaret hesitated over a word she corrected her gently and without that quick irritability which so often expressed itself when she thought someone was being stupid or unintelligent.

Andora found that the story could not hold her attention and she began to daydream, remembering how last night Mistress Blanche Parry had told her fortune.

'You will find happiness, dear,' she said. 'A dark, handsome man will reach for your heart. You will fall in love and such love will last until you die. But . . .'

She paused a minute, peering over the

cards with her old, short-sighted eyes until Andora grew apprehensive, even though she told herself it was all for amusement and she did not believe one half of the fortunes Mistress Parry doled out so glibly to all the Maids-of-Honour.

'What do you see?' she cried. 'Is it bad news?'

Her thoughts winged their way to her father. Suppose he were really ill and she was not with him? She often wondered whether anyone realised how frail he was.

'There are strange things here,' Mistress Parry said peering at the knave of clubs. 'There is some obstacle . . . to be overcome before you find happiness, child. I see a shadow across your path — nay, more than a shadow, it is . . . blood . . . danger . . . and death!'

The old woman spoke in a low, muttering tone, almost as if she was talking to herself; and then, with a start, she looked up and saw Andora's startled eyes and said quickly:

'What am I saying? It is ridiculous. Of course I see none of those things. I was but talking to myself as an old woman does far too easily. There is nothing but happiness in the cards for you, child — happiness and a long life and plenty of money.'

Andora had risen from the table feeling as

if a cold hand was clutching at her heart. She was not deceived for a moment by Mistress Parry's glib assurances. When she had spoken in that low, muttering voice, she had been seeing the truth or what she believed to be the truth. What she was saying now was only the fortune-telling that she doled out so readily to the other girls who plagued her at all times of the day and night.

'He looked at me and smiled, Mistress Parry,' one would cry. 'Tell me quickly, is he in love with me?'

While another would say:

'I have bought a new gown. Will it bring me luck?'

Questions like these were to be heard daily in the Maids-of-Honours' sitting-room and Andora knew only too well by the tone of her voice what Mistress Parry's answers would be. She promised luck and love and for all of them marriage to the man of their heart. But when she had spoken of death and blood it had been in a very different tone. There was something about her, something which Andora could only describe to herself as fey.

Perhaps Sir Hengist was right, she thought, and it was better not to dabble too deeply in things which were best left to men rather than women. And yet, if Lord Burleigh was to be believed, the Queen's life was in danger if there was, indeed, a spy in the most intimate Court circles.

Andora let her mind run over the people she had met since she had come to the Palace. At first there had seemed a vast concourse of them; but gradually, as she had got to know them better, she found there were not, in truth, so very many who were in daily contact with the Queen or were likely to overhear the discussions or decisions of the Privy Council.

Besides the statesmen themselves there were the gentlemen in attendance on Lord Essex and the Gentlemen-at-Arms, who had the privilege of forming the Queen's personal bodyguard. These were all members of families which had served the Crown loyally for generations, like Lord Murton, whose father had been in attendance on the Queen's father, Henry VIII.

Andora had begun to know them all by sight. Some were old, some were very young, and yet she could swear that every one of them was devoted heart and soul to the Queen's Majesty and ready to fight and die for her at any time should it be required of them.

After her experience with Lord Braye she had tried not to be suspicious of anyone.

She had realised what a fool she had made of herself and knew that common sense was what she needed rather than a zealous fanaticism which suspected treachery in every word and in every gesture from people who, when investigated, were not in the least likely to prove treacherous.

She could not help thinking that if, indeed, information was being given to the enemy, it came from one of the many servants who moved about the Palace apparently unnoticed. Without letting it appear that she was interested, she had questioned Lady Howard about this, who, as Keeper of the Queen's Jewels, had a sentry stationed outside her apartments.

'Might there not be thieves, Madam, amongst the hundreds of servants there are in the Palace? How do we know when new ones arrive that they have not been placed there by persons who have designs upon Her Majesty's wealth, if not on more serious things like the secrets of State?'

'Such ideas have worried wiser heads than yours,' Lady Howard answered. 'All the servants in the Queen's apartments are known personally to the Comptroller. They have either served in the Royal Household for generations or else, if someone new is engaged, he makes the closest enquiries about

167

them — where they come from, their home life, their relations and whether the references they bring when applying for the post are impeccable in every way.'

'What about the servants of all the noblemen and ladies of the Court?'

'Those, of course, are outside our control,' Lady Howard said. 'But they would find it very difficult to enter the Queen's apartments without being observed. I assure you, Mistress Bland, there are eyes as well as ears everywhere in this part of the Palace.'

Andora had felt reassured. At the same time, it was no answer to Lord Burleigh's query as to how the Queen's secrets had been carried to France ahead of the official Royal messenger. Lord Burleigh could not have been mistaken; and, as he had said, it was not once nor even twice, but continually that news was seeping out and being made known abroad before the Queen had agreed that a messenger should be despatched.

And the question was, of course, how much more information that they did not know about was escaping from the Palace? How many secrets of Elizabeth's Army and Navy had already reached the ears of Philip of Spain?

It seemed to Andora that the Spanish King was like some great spider drawing people into his web and enmeshing them so that they could not escape but must toil for him as he worked unceasingly for the downfall of England and her Queen.

Andora must have fallen asleep for suddenly she was dreaming that she was in Spain and Philip was reaching out his arms towards her, drawing her irresistibly towards him, and though she struggled and strove she could not escape him. She could feel herself being carried nearer and nearer until she could see the expression on his face and it was that of a demon . . .

It was then, with a little shudder which seemed to shake her whole body, that she woke up. For a moment she was not certain where she was, but as she saw the sunlight glinting through the window on her white gown, she heard a man's voice say:

'The Fleet weighed anchor on 1st June. Sir Francis escorted us west to the Cape and then, as we turned northward, Your Majesty, he sailed out into the open Atlantic towards the setting sun.'

'He must have changed his plans,' the Queen said, her voice sharp. 'In his last letter he wrote that he was staying near the Cape of Saint Vincent. Read the Admiral what Sir Francis said.'

Andora heard the rustle of papers and then Sir Francis Walsingham's voice, low and deep, reading aloud:

'As long as it shall please God to give us provisions to eat and drink and that our ships and wind and weather will permit us, you shall shortly hear of us near this Cape of Saint Vincent where we desire and will expect daily what Her Majesty and Your Honour will further command. God make us all thankful that Her Majesty sent out these few ships in time.'

'That was written on the twenty-fourth day of May,' the Queen interposed. 'What made Sir Francis change his mind?'

'He did not confide in me, Your Majesty,' the Admiral answered. 'But methinks a prisoner who was persuaded to talk on our homeward voyage may have the key to the enigma.'

'What did he say?' Elizabeth asked eagerly.

'He said, Your Majesty, that King Philip was afraid that Sir Francis Drake would hear of the *San Filipe*.'

'The *San Filipe*! What is that? A man-o'-war?'

'No, indeed!' Lord Burleigh interposed. Andora knew his quiet, statesmanlike voice. 'The *San Filipe* is a carrack — one of the largest in the whole of the Spanish Fleet. This time of year it is homeward bound from Goa with the annual cargo of spices and Oriental goods from Portugal's Eastern Empire.'

'A valuable cargo? One that would be worth the taking?' the Queen enquired.

'Valuable indeed!' Lord Burleigh replied. 'From the reports of men who know what the *San Filipe* usually carries, her holds are stuffed with pepper, cinnamon and cloves, calicoes, silks and ivory, besides a vast quantity of gold, silver and caskets of jewels.'

'God's teeth! If Sir Francis should capture her it would be a prize indeed!' the Queen cried.

'It would, Your Majesty,' Sir Francis Walsingham agreed.

'Then we can but pray that Sir Francis has taken his Fleet out into the Atlantic because he has wind of this treasure ship,' Elizabeth said. 'We have put our trust in him before, gentlemen, and he has never failed us. We must go down on our knees to ask that he will not do so this time.'

With a sudden sense of dismay Andora

realised that she was eavesdropping. She had felt so stupefied when she had first awoken from her nightmare that she had listened to the voices at the other end of the room without being aware of what she was doing. And now, fully awake and looking around, she saw that the Maids-of-Honour had all withdrawn, as was usual when Her Majesty gave a private audience. No one would be aware of her presence because she was seated behind a large cabinet of ebony inset with ivory which jutted out into the room and effectually concealed her.

She heard the Admiral being dismissed; then, as the door closed behind him, she rose to her feet and appeared from behind the cabinet. The Queen gave a sudden exclamation:

'The devil take it! What are you doing there, child?'

'I must beg Your Majesty's pardon, but I fell asleep,' Andora explained.

'Mistress Parry should have seen that you left with the others,' the Queen said angrily. 'Am I never to be served with any efficiency?'

'Pray do not blame Mistress Parry, Your Majesty,' Andora begged. 'It was entirely my own fault.'

'How much have you overheard?' Lord Burleigh asked.

'I heard what the Admiral reported of Sir Francis Drake's movements,' Andora said with a flush mounting on her cheeks. 'I know now that I should have spoken at once, but I was bewildered after a strange dream and I listened almost without realising that I was doing so.'

Lord Burleigh put his hand on her shoulder.

'You realise that what you overheard is of the utmost importance to the Queen and to England?' he said. 'Should the spies of Spain know where Sir Francis Drake has gone, they might send out ships to intercept him and not only prevent him from capturing this great prize but overwhelm his small fleet and stop his ever returning to us.'

'You know I would die rather than relate what I have heard,' Andora answered.

'You speak like your father's daughter,' Lord Burleigh said. He looked towards the Queen.

'Yes, yes, we can trust her,' Elizabeth said testily. 'But another time, Mistress Bland, do not fall asleep when you are on duty. The Bible tells us that only foolish virgins do that.'

'I promise Your Majesty to be more circumspect,' Andora said, curtsying.

She escaped from the room feeling that

she had been let off very lightly, only to be scolded ferociously by Mistress Parry.

'Falling asleep, indeed!' she snorted. 'I have never heard of such a thing. It is lucky for you the Queen has not punished you for such impertinence. Do not let it occur again or I promise you you will certainly have me to reckon with.'

Andora was not afraid of Mistress Parry, none of them were. She was, in fact, far too easy-going with the Maids-of-Honour. It was hard to keep refusing to meet Lord Murton at the many assignations he suggested when all the other Maids-of-Honour were having clandestine meetings and flirting outrageously with noblemen, who passed them notes under Mistress Parry's very nose.

Finally, the following day, because she could think of no further excuses, Andora found herself down by the river alone with Lord Murton.

The Queen had gone riding and it was an accepted custom at the Palace that when the cat was away the mice would play. It was one thing to think that one would sit sewing or reading, as they were all supposed to do in the heat of the afternoon. But it was quite another thing to be the only person doing it, to be laughed at and teased by the other

Maids-of-Honour or even to be called a little prig because the others resented that she should be serious while they were frivolous.

'You have come at last,' Lord Murton said when he met her, as he had suggested, under the shade of the great sycamore tree.

'I . . . I cannot stay . . . long,' Andora said a little nervously.

'Do not be afraid,' he answered. 'Her Majesty will be riding for several hours this afternoon.'

'Who told you that?' Andora enquired.

'One of Lord Essex's gentlemen,' he replied. 'I made the enquiry so that I should know how long I could be alone with you, Andora. You have been so cruel and distant with me that I must count the minutes that I may spend with you.'

'Pray do not send me so many letters,' Andora said primly. 'It is embarrassing. The others tease me.'

'I would not embarrass you for all the world,' he answered. 'And yet, at the same time, I want to tell everyone that I love you. You are so beautiful, Andora. Smile at me. Let me see the dimples in your cheeks.'

She could not help smiling at the insistence in his voice. He was very handsome, she thought. Mistress Parry's words came back to her.

'A dark, handsome man will reach for your heart.'

Lord Murton was certainly dark and handsome, but when he tried to cover her hand with kisses Andora drew it away from him.

'Someone might see us,' she said nervously.

'Let us go from here,' he suggested. 'There is a seat in the Water Garden which is sheltered and where we can talk.'

She let him lead her into one of the beautiful little formal gardens enclosed by a privet hedge where the ornamental water was surrounded by yellow iris and covered by the great green leaves of water-lilies.

'No one will see us here,' Lord Murton smiled.

It did, indeed, seem safe and private and Andora relaxed a little. She did not know why, but she was afraid of being alone with Lord Murton. She was afraid of being seen and afraid of something else which she could not even put into words.

'The first time I saw you,' Lord Murton said, 'I knew that you were the woman I had been looking for for years — no, for all my life. You were looking lost that night,

Andora; lost but so lovely that my heart flew from my breast and has been in your keeping ever since.'

'And yet you nearly got me into trouble,' Andora told him. 'If I had gone into the garden with you, I might not be here now.'

'It was wrong of me,' he replied. 'But your loveliness drove me crazy. I forgot everything but that I wanted to be alone with you, to tell you that I had fallen in love for the first and last time in my life.'

'How can you be sure of that?' Andora asked with a smile.

'I am sure,' he answered. 'I have thought that I loved many women, Andora. I am twenty-five years of age so you will not expect me to tell you otherwise. But this is the first time in my whole life that I have been really in love. I cannot sleep for thinking of you. I cannot eat. I live only to see you, and yet every day goes by and you will not come.'

'It is impossible. Do you not understand? I am here to serve Her Majesty.'

'So are the other Maids-of-Honour and they do not find it impossible to meet their friends.'

'I . . . I . . .' Andora began, then hesitated.

She had been about to say: 'I am different,' and then knew that such a remark would be dangerous.

177

'Well?' he asked as she did not speak. 'You see, you have no real excuse. Andora, be kind to me. You are making me so unhappy, so utterly miserable.'

'I would not wish to do that,' Andora said, touched by the warm note in his voice.

'Then let us meet at least once a day,' Lord Murton begged. 'You do not know what hell it is to see you across the dance floor, or standing behind Her Majesty's chair in the Audience Chamber, and know that I cannot touch you, cannot tell you how much you mean to me.'

'You must not love me so much,' Andora said.

'That is something I cannot help,' Lord Murton replied. 'Andora, will you marry me?'

She did not answer and after a moment he went on:

'I should not ask you this. There are reasons why my family do not wish me to marry for the present. And yet I know that I cannot live without you. Marry me secretly and then when things are a little easier at home we will tell your parents and my father.'

Andora pulled her hand away from his.

'I think, my Lord,' she said, 'that such a suggestion is insulting. I have no intention of marrying anyone, and I assure you I would marry no one in secret without my parents' consent.'

Lord Murton got to his feet and stood for a moment looking out towards the river. His face was very pale and she saw that he was breathing agitatedly. Then suddenly he turned and threw himself on his knees before her.

'If that is so, say you will marry me and I will ride tonight to your father and ask his permission. It is no use, Andora, I cannot live without you. If your father will accept me as his future son-in-law, then I will tell my father and force him to agree. Nothing else matters — nothing.'

'Please get up,' Andora begged. 'I am very sensible, my Lord, of the honour that you are according me, but I must have time to think. I do not know you. I know nothing about you. Indeed, until this moment I did not even know that your father was alive.'

Lord Murton gave a deep sigh and resumed his seat beside her.

'I thought someone might have told you,' he said. 'My father quarrelled with Lord Burleigh fifteen years ago over some trivial matter — I do not think either of them remember what it was — but he stalked out of the Palace and said he would never return. He never has.'

He smiled at her and took her hand again.

'He is the Earl of Thanet,' he went on, 'and he lives a very quiet life in a Castle on our estates. My mother, who has since died, was an invalid for years so she never missed the gaiety of the Court although when at first they went into my father's self-imposed exile she grumbled because in those days she was a very beautiful woman.'

'What a strange story,' Andora exclaimed.

'Not a very interesting one,' Lord Murton said quickly. 'That is why I have never spoken of my parents before. Apart from that, I am an only child. And now you know all there is to know about me. Please give me your answer.'

'I cannot,' Andora answered. 'I like you. I think you are . . . very nice. But, I . . . I do not know you well enough to even think of you as . . .' She hesitated for the word.

'Your husband?' Lord Murton suggested. 'Oh, Andora, do not keep me waiting. Do not leave me in these torments of hell in which I am now. I want you. I want you to belong to me, to be mine — my wife, my life, my love.'

He spoke with so much ardour and passion that almost instinctively Andora rose to her feet.

'Please, my Lord, let us try and be friends,' she pleaded. 'I will meet you when it is possible so that we can get to know each other better, but it is far too soon to talk of anything else. When I fall in love — if ever I do — I hope it will be with somebody whom I can love for the whole of my life. There is, therefore, no need to hurry over such an important decision.'

'You do not know what love means,' Lord Murton said despairingly.

He stood beside her, looking down at her little face raised to his.

'You are so small, Andora,' he said, 'and yet in your tiny hands you hold my whole life, my only hope of happiness.'

Quite suddenly he put his arms around her.

'Love me a little,' he said. 'Only a very little, and give me a glimpse of Heaven. I love you so desperately.'

There was at that moment something pathetic about him, and because Andora did not force him away from her with an exclamation of anger, he drew her closer still and before she could prevent it bent his head and found her lips.

She felt the full passion of his desire for her and the hunger of his mouth as he held her tightly to him, and for a moment, because she was taken by surprise and because her pity for him superseded all else, she did not struggle.

'I love you! Oh, God, I love you!' he muttered, and then suddenly they both started as a voice behind them said sarcastically:

'A very pretty scene!'

Andora disengaged herself from Lord Murton's arms and turned to see Sir Hengist glowering down at them, his grey eyes like steel, his red hair almost like fire as it glinted in the sun's rays. She had the sudden absurd thought that he was like an avenging angel, and then felt the colour rush crimson into her cheeks as he said:

'I rescued you once, Andora, from the unwelcome attentions of a gentleman. Must I do so again?'

'What the hell are you doing here?' Lord Murton asked angrily. 'Cannot you keep out of my way?'

'Nothing would please me better,' Sir Hengist replied. 'But my business is not with you but with Mistress Bland.'

'The Queen has returned?' Andora asked nervously.

'Her Majesty returned about ten minutes ago,' Sir Hengist said. 'One of the Royal party was thrown from his horse and broke a leg, so they returned home. There were no

Maids-of-Honour to be found anywhere. You had best have an explanation ready.'

'I will go to Her Majesty at once,' Andora said, agitatedly lifting her skirt.

'I will show you the quickest way,' Sir Hengist said in an abrupt, uncompromising tone which told her all too clearly what his feelings were towards her.

She felt her heart sink, but there was no time to worry about anything but what explanation she should give the Queen.

'I am sorry, Andora, if I have got you into trouble,' Lord Murton said in a low voice.

'It is something you seem singularly adept at contriving to do,' Sir Hengist remarked aggressively.

'I was not speaking to you,' Lord Murton retorted rudely.

'If I gave you your deserts, Murton,' Sir Hengist said, 'I would challenge you to a duel or give you the soundest thrashing you have ever had in your life. But if I fought you I should kill you, and if I thrashed you I should be merely exerting myself to no purpose. You cannot train a dog that is untrainable.'

Lord Murton stepped forward with fury in his face.

'How dare you speak to me in such a manner?' he stormed.

'I dare and I shall dare a great deal more if you do not get out of our way,' Sir Hengist said. 'Mistress Bland will be late.'

He pushed Lord Murton to one side and putting his hand under Andora's elbow hurried her up the path, leading her along a twisting, turning route through walled gardens and secret paths until panting a little, she exclaimed:

'It is a long way back to the Palace.'

'It is, the way I am taking you,' he replied.

'But we must hurry!' Andora exclaimed.

'Not really,' he answered.

She looked up at him in astonishment.

'What do you mean?' she asked, a sudden suspicion crossing her mind.

He stopped in his tracks and turned round to face her.

'The Queen has not returned,' he said, 'so you need not think of an explanation for your conduct — except to me.'

'You mean you lied?' Andora asked.

'If you call saving you from the attentions of that unpleasant fellow a lie,' Sir Hengist replied.

'But you frightened me,' Andora said accusingly. 'I believed you. I thought you were telling the truth.'

'What do you mean by being down there with him?' Sir Hengist enquired.

'What right have you to question me?' Andora asked, angry now because she had been so frightened and conscious of an acute embarrassment because he had actually seen Lord Murton kissing her.

'Have you no shame?' he asked. 'Would you let every lovesick fool maul you as he was doing?'

'That is not true!' Andora cried. 'No one else has kissed me save Lord Braye — if you call that kissing — and I do not really know why I let Lord Murton, save that he asked me to marry him.'

'Marry him! What did you answer?'

'What is that to do with you?' Andora asked.

'You little fool, you are playing with fire,' Sir Hengist said. 'Men like Murton are not to be trusted. I do not suppose for a moment that he means actually to marry you.'

'But he asked me,' Andora said, stung by the contempt in his tone.

'Talking is one thing, action is another,' Sir Hengist said cynically.

'He asked me; but whether he did or whether he did not has nothing to do with you,' Andora said. 'You have no right to make trouble by being rude to him and enticing me away from his company with lies.

You are not my keeper.'

'If I were, you would behave in a very different manner from the way you are behaving now, making yourself cheap by flirtations of this sort.'

His words stung into her and she felt an anger which surpassed anything she had ever known before. She stamped her foot and stormed at him:

'Go away and leave me alone! Do not interfere in my life. You have no right and you make everything sordid, horrible and beastly. It was not like that — and even if it had been, it is no business of yours. I hate you! I hate you!'

Her hands were clenched, her head was thrown back defiantly. He seemed so large, so overpowering, and yet she felt that in her anger she could have felled him to the ground.

'I will certainly do my best to keep out of your way in future,' Sir Hengist retorted furiously. 'But if it is kisses you want, then they are easy enough to get. And you might as well get them from a man who knows how to give them.'

He spoke between clenched teeth, and before she could realise what was happening he had swept her into his arm and his mouth was on hers, holding her utterly captive. She felt as if he squeezed the breath out of her body, and at the same time he drew her very soul from between her lips.

Then before she could struggle or attempt to cry out, before she could even move, he had flung her from him so violently that she would have fallen had she not supported herself against the trunk of a tree.

Without another word and without looking back he walked away from her down the tree-shaded path and disappeared, leaving her completely alone.

8

Andora put up her hands to her burning cheeks. Had this really happened to her? Could Sir Hengist really have kissed her? How dare he behave in such a manner? And yet somehow she was no longer angry with him, only perilously near to tears.

She had a sudden panic that he might return and she would have to face him again. Picking up her skirt, she sped like a frightened animal down the long walk, under the trees, and at the end of it discovered a rose garden which she recognised. Hurrying through it, she found her way back to the Palace.

She ran upstairs and was just about to enter her own bedchamber when she heard someone call her name. She turned to see Lady Mary Howard standing in the doorway of the sitting-room.

Lady Mary was still in disgrace and confined to her own bedchamber and the room where the other Maids-of-Honour sat when they were off duty.

'Andora,' she called now. 'Come and talk to me for pity's sake or I shall go crazed, sitting here by myself, knowing nothing, hearing nothing, seeing nothing.'

'I am sorry . . . Mary . . .' Andora began to say, thinking quickly of an excuse so that she could be alone. And then she realised how selfish she was being and reluctantly crossed the passage to enter the big, sunlit room which overlooked the river.

'Where have you been?' Lady Mary began in conversational tone. Then she said quickly: 'Something is wrong. You are upset, Andora. You are trembling.'

'It is nothing,' Andora answered. 'Nothing at all.'

'Nonsense!' Lady Mary retorted. 'I can believe the evidence of my own eyes. What has happened, Andora? Please tell me.'

'It is nothing,' Andora repeated, walking to the window to look out on to the shining river.

'It is Lord Murton,' Lady Mary said accusingly. 'What has he said to you? Has he not made you an offer?'

'Yes, he has,' Andora admitted unwillingly.

It was some relief, at any rate, that Mary Howard had not guessed the real cause of her agitation.

'He has proposed!' Lady Mary exclaimed excitedly. 'Oh, Andora, did you accept him?'

'No, of course not,' Andora said. 'Why, I have barely made his acquaintance. How could I love someone I have known such a short time?'

Lady Mary sighed.

'That shows you are not in love, although you might do worse than become my Lady Murton. He is rich, he is charming, he is *persona grata* at Court. The Queen was saying a week or so ago what perfect manners he has.'

'One cannot marry for good manners,' Andora said almost sharply.

'No, one can only marry for love,' Lady Mary said dreamily. 'It is quite plain, Andora, that you are not in love or you would not talk about not knowing the person for a long or a short time. When one falls in love it happens in the flicker of an eyelid; in the hesitation between one word and another.'

Andora turned from the window and looked at Lady Mary, so small and pretty, her dark hair framing the oval of her face and her blue eyes with a strange, mysterious expression in them as if she looked inward at her own feelings.

'Tell me, Mary,' she said, crossing the room to sit down near her, 'how does one feel when one is in love?'

Lady Mary Howard laced her white fingers together.

'I cannot put it into words,' she answered. 'As you know, Andora, poets have tried to do that since the beginning of time and have failed.'

'What do you feel at first?' Andora asked.

'I think it is a sudden awareness of the person one loves,' Lady Mary replied. 'He seems to stand out, too, as if he were the central figure in every room, in every scene, and everyone else fades into insignificance. And then, when he comes near you, you feel a sudden tingling, a sudden excitement, which seems to agitate every nerve in your body. Your heart begins to thump, your breath comes quickly between your lips. You feel frightened and tense, yet, at the same time, happy with the joyfulness beyond words. Above all, you ache for him to touch you.'

'And when he touches you?' Andora asked.

'Then you are caught up into Heaven itself,' Lady Mary whispered.

'But how do you know this?' Andora enquired. 'You are in love with Lord Essex, but you do not even know him. You have never been alone with him.'

Lady Mary glanced over her shoulder towards the closed door.

'If I tell you a secret which no one else knows, will you promise never to reveal it to anyone?' she asked.

'I promise,' Andora reassured her.

'Then I will tell you. He has kissed me. I have felt his lips on mine and I gave him my heart.' Lady Mary gave a little sigh. 'Indeed, I would have given him more had he asked it of me.'

'Mary!' Andora ejaculated in a shocked voice.

'Yes, yes, I know all the things you would say to me,' Lady Mary said. 'I know all the arguments about purity, decency and keeping oneself immaculate for one's husband. But, Andora, I love him! I want him for my husband.'

'Mary, you are crazed!' Andora ejaculated. 'My Lord Essex belongs to the Queen. It is sacrilege for you even to think of him as a man, let alone as a lover. I have not been long in the Court, but I know how dangerous it is for you to speak of him in this way.'

There was silence for a moment as Lady Mary did not answer and then, because her curiosity was too much for her, Andora said:

'When did you get the chance of meeting him alone? Of letting him kiss you? I thought he never left the Queen's side.'

'It was the first night he arrived,' Lady Mary said dreamily. 'He came from the country, unknown and unheralded. There was a Ball that night and in between the dances we moved about the Palace, sitting first in this room and then in another, and a lot of people, unbeknown to Her Majesty, disappeared upstairs into the bedchambers. There were so many present that it was impossible to keep track of anyone in particular.'

'Yes, go on. What happened?' Andora prompted.

'I was standing alone for a moment because my partner had left me to procure a glass of wine,' Lady Mary said, 'when I saw this tall, handsome young man standing alone, looking a little ill at ease. Feeling kindly and sympathetic because I have known what it was to feel shy and awkward at Court, I went up to him and said: "You are new here. Would you like me to find you a partner for the next dance?" "Will you accord me that honour?" he enquired.'

Lady Mary paused a moment before she said in a soft voice:

'I can see the look in his eyes now and the smile on his lips. Oh, Andora, he was the most handsome man I had ever seen in the whole of my life.'

'So you danced with him,' Andora said. 'And afterwards?'

'We found a little room lined with books where we sat and talked about ourselves. He told me his name and how anxious he was to serve the Queen. I wanted him to go on talking all night. I wanted to go on listening to him. I wanted to be near him.'

Lady Mary put her hands up to her eyes for a moment as if to shut out everything else by the memory of that evening.

'At last he said he thought we ought to go back to the Ballroom and when he opened the door we could hear the music coming up the stairs to where we were. He laughed and said: "Will you dance with me again?" and we danced together in the empty room with only the books to watch us. I felt as if I were floating in a dream.'

'I cannot understand why nobody missed you,' Andora said.

'As I have said, there were so many people in the Palace. I was not on duty that night. I was wearing a new gown of red velvet trimmed with fur and I knew it became me as no other gown has ever done.'

'What happened when the dance finished?' Andora asked.

Lady Mary shut her eyes, her long, dark eyelashes sweeping against her pale cheeks.

'As the music finished he did not let go of my hand but drew me nearer to him. I made no pretence of resisting, Andora. I knew that he was about to kiss me. I wanted his kiss more than I have ever wanted anything in the whole of my life.'

' "You are so small and pretty," he said.' Lady Mary's voice deepened and with a little sob she went on: 'He kissed me and I knew that I loved him — loved him madly, frantically, completely.'

'It happened just like that! You are sure? Quite sure?' Andora asked in a puzzled voice.

'As sure as I am that Elizabeth sits on the Throne of England,' Lady Mary answered. 'It was not something one could question or wonder about. It was just a fact. I loved him and I belonged to him completely should he care to take me.'

'What happened then?'

'We had to go back to the Ballroom. We had no sooner reached it than my Lord Burleigh came up to Lord Essex to say that the Queen had heard of his arrival and asked that he should be presented to her. He was

195

taken away from me, Andora. I have never been close to him again.'

'But surely he has noticed you standing behind Her Majesty? Surely he has made some sign to show you that he has not forgotten that you danced together, that he kissed you?'

Lady Mary sighed.

'For a week after the night of the Ball I was laid low with a fever. I was forced to keep to my own bedchamber. Mistress Parry would not let me leave it even though I assured her that nothing was wrong.'

Lady Mary clenched her hands together.

'I swear that woman ruined my life! When I rejoined the others, it was too late.'

'He had forgotten you,' Andora said softly.

'No, the Queen had bewitched him,' Lady Mary replied harshly. 'And that is the right word, Andora. She is a witch. She is not an ordinary woman. What ordinary woman of her age could attract a young man of twenty-three? She uses witchcraft to bind him to her. I have heard tales of strange rites that take place in her chamber when she is alone at night.'

Andora laughed. She could not help it.

'Oh, really, Mary! You do not believe those stories, you know you did not. They are invented by the Spaniards who spread the most wicked lies about Her Majesty, as we well know. My father says it is a compliment that they should be so vitriolic, for it means that they are afraid both of the Queen and of England.'

'Everyone is afraid of her!' Mary exclaimed. 'They would be foolish if they were not. After all, she has the power of life and death. But that does not account for the way Lord Essex looks at her, the way he seems to tremble when she touches him. I have seen them together, Andora. There is not a glance that they have given each other which has not been like a sword thrust in my heart.'

'Oh, poor, poor Mary! I am so sorry for you,' Andora said.

'Be sorry for yourself,' Lady Mary retorted. 'And for all women who love men. For love can bring one nothing but misery.'

'That is not true,' Andora said quietly. 'I know it is not true.'

'No, not entirely,' Lady Mary agreed, her voice throbbing. 'It can be an ecstasy as well. When he kissed me, I felt as if my whole body had wings, that I was flying upwards into the very heart of the burning sun. Now can you understand why I still want him, why I lie awake night after night craving his kisses and the feel of his mouth on mine?'

Lady Mary's voice broke on the last word and she started to cry; helpless, despairing tears which rolled down her cheeks to fall on her hands, clenched in her lap so tightly that the fingers showed white.

Swiftly, because she could never bear to see suffering, Andora knelt at her side and put her arms around her.

'Oh, Mary, I am so sorry,' she said. 'If only there was something I could do, my dearest. But I promise you that writing him notes will do more harm than good while he cares only for the Queen. He will either laugh at them or betray you, which would be even more disastrous.'

'I think I would rather face the block than go on suffering as I have these past months,' Lady Mary sobbed.

'This is foolish talk,' Andora told her. 'You are young, you are beautiful. There are other men in the world besides Lord Essex.'

'I know,' Lady Mary answered miserably. 'There are many men nearly as handsome and perhaps just as attractive to other women — but not to me. As far as I am concerned there is only one man.'

She put up her hands to her eyes.

'One day you will feel like that, Andora. You will know that because of a man's kiss and the touch of his hand you are willing to sacrifice everything, even life itself, if only you could be near him for a little while.'

Lady Mary sighed and gave herself a shake.

'And now we have talked enough about me,' she said in a different tone. 'You are so kind and sympathetic, Andora, that I have thought only of my troubles and not of yours. It was you who were perturbed when you came into this room, not me.'

'Thinking of you has made my own troubles sink into insignificance,' Andora said quickly, hoping she would escape further questioning.

'What did Lord Murton say when he proposed?' Lady Mary asked. 'Did he kiss you?'

Andora got to her feet and walked to the window again.

'I would rather not speak of it,' she said.

'Then he did,' Lady Mary cried almost gleefully. 'It is no use pretending, Andora. Your face is far too transparent. I do not believe you have ever told a lie willingly in the whole of your life. He kissed you, did he not?'

'I am not going to answer that question,' Andora retorted.

'Then I know he did,' Lady Mary said, 'otherwise you would deny it. Was it your first kiss? What did you feel? A sudden throbbing in your temples; a feeling of suffocation in your throat; and then a flame coming to life within you — a flame that grows, leaps higher and higher until you feel as if it must consume both you and him?'

'No, no, I felt nothing like that,' Andora replied. 'I beg you, Mary, not to speak of it further. I . . . I cannot bear it!'

Without explanation or excuse she ran across the room, pulled open the door and without bothering to close it behind her, slipped across the passage and into her own bedchamber. There she thrust the bolt in place and threw herself down on the bed.

For a moment she lay still, her face hidden in the pillow, her whole body tense, her fingers clenched in the palms of her hands. Then, after some minutes, she began to wonder what Lady Mary must think of her for running away like that. It was rude, and yet she could not explain how the other girl's questions were torturing her, how hard it was to answer or, harder still to prevaricate and avoid the truth.

For though she felt she would rather die than admit it, it was not with Lord Murton that she had felt the feelings which Lady

Mary had described so vividly, but with Sir Hengist!

She could hardly believe it and yet the truth leapt out at her vividly, as if she saw it written on the wall. Lord Murton's kiss had meant nothing to her, had evoked no response within herself and aroused no emotion save that of pity. But it was Sir Hengist's lips which had awoken within her a flame which seemed to leap upwards within her body. It was Sir Hengist who seemed to draw her heart from between her lips.

'It cannot be true!' Andora said aloud, and yet she knew it was the truth. She was in love with a man who despised her, a man she hated!

In another part of the Palace another woman was thinking at that moment of Sir Hengist and speaking of him with her servant.

'You are sure, Harry, that you are not mistaken?' she asked one of her pages.

'No, indeed, m'Lady. I saw them go into the shrubbery together. They crossed the herb garden and Sir Hengist held Mistress Bland by the arm.'

'Where had they been?' Lady Malvern asked sharply.

'They seemed to come from the direction

of the river, m'Lady.'

'They were alone? You are quite certain they were alone?'

'Absolutely, m'Lady. There was no one about, no one else at all.'

Lady Malvern's eyes narrowed. This was intolerable, she told herself. Sir Hengist, it was true, had paid little attention to her since her arrival at Court; but she had thought it was because he was required to be constantly in attendance on Lord Essex. If he had time to philander with the Queen's Maids-of-Honour, it was time she looked to her laurels.

She dismissed the page and walked restlessly up and down her sitting-room, the silken skirts of her gown making a soft frou-frou over the polished boards, the jewels on her fingers and round her wrists glittering in the sunshine as she moved.

She must do something and do it at once, she told herself. But it was a little difficult to know what. She had already invited Sir Hengist to supper only to be told that his duties made it impossible for him to know from hour to hour when he would be free.

He was charming when they met in public; and although she told herself that he held her hand a little longer than was necessary and looked at her with a special light in his eyes, she could not be certain that it was not her imagination. She had the suspicion that he was just as polite and charming to the other ladies of the Court.

'He shall not escape me!' she said aloud through gritted teeth, and remembered how different he had been in what seemed those very far-off days before she had been forced to go to the country and leave everything that amused and interested her behind.

Then she had held him enthralled, as she had held half-a-dozen other young men. He was not so sure of himself in those days and perhaps he had been grateful for her interest in him.

She remembered their clandestine meetings; those nights when she had crept out after her husband was asleep to meet him in the dark galleries or in one of the numerous anterooms. The Court had been at Hampton Palace at the time and it had been easy to escape observation there and in the spacious gardens.

She remembered a little arbour covered in honeysuckle and a waning moon being obscured by clouds. The thought of what had happened in the darkness made Lilian Malvern draw in her breath quickly.

Then suddenly she had a plan. She moved across the room with a quick sense of urgency to peal the bell for one of her long-suffering servants.

'Bring parchment, a fresh quill and sand,' she said curtly, 'and make haste about it or there will be change in this household before long.'

She stood waiting, tapping her foot on the boards, until another servant appeared in the doorway.

'What is it?' Lady Malvern enquired.

'Master Julian Kirk is here, m'Lady.'

'Again!' Lilian Malvern exclaimed. 'Did you tell him I was not at home?'

'I told him, m'Lady, as you had instructed me. He said he would wait until you returned. Nothing will persuade him to leave.'

'Then drive him away!' Lilian Malvern declared hysterically. 'Beat him! Whip him! Throw stones at him! Do anything you like, but persuade him to stop pestering me. Tell him, as I have told him myself, that I have no further use for him.'

'Yes, m'Lady.'

The servant bowed and withdrew and Lilian Malvern dismissed Julian Kirk from her mind as, a moment later, she sat down to pen a note.

When it was finished she left it lying on the table and sent for her maid.

'I want to change my gown.'

'You will require a ballgown, m'Lady?'

'No, you fool. I want a negligée, something soft and clinging and feminine. What have I got?'

The woman hesitated.

'There is your black.'

'Black!' Lilian Malvern exclaimed. 'Use your brains, woman, if you have any. Is it likely, after wearing black for a year, that I should wish to wear it now? No, no, there must be something else.'

'There is the pink lace, m'Lady. But . . . do you remember?'

'Yes, of course, the pink,' Lady Malvern said. 'Yet what should I remember?'

'That when his Lordship was alive he said it was far too indecent for a respectable lady.'

'Yes, of course, I recall it now. That is, indeed, the gown I require,' Lady Malvern said. 'Fetch it out — and the devil take you if it is not fresh and recently pressed.'

It was not to her Ladyship's liking, of course, and her maid was in tears long before she was bathed and dressed and bedecked with a long row of jewels which did little to hide the inadequacy of the bodice.

'How think you?' my Lady Malvern asked looking at herself in the mirror.

'You look very beautiful, m'Lady,' the

maid replied, as was expected of her. 'But . . .'

'But what, you idiot?' Lilian Malvern enquired.

'You could not allow Her Majesty to see you in this.'

Lady Malvern threw back her head and laughed.

'Her Majesty will not see me,' she said. 'You can make certain of that. I want a decanter of the very best wine we have brought to my sitting-room. Close the curtains, light the candles and scent the room with herbs.'

'Yes, m'Lady.'

The maid withdrew and Lilian Malvern posed her body first this way and then that way, watching the effect in the mirror. There was no doubt at all that the negligée was daring, almost to the point of impropriety. No man could look at her, she thought, and his passions remain unaroused, unawakened, at the sight of so much beauty so subtly and so gloriously revealed.

She looked round her bedchamber. In the big, oak, four-poster the lace-edged sheets scented with lavender which she had brought from the country had been changed that very morning. The pillows were spotless, the silk embroidered curtains hanging from the canopy were a promise of secrecy. She walked across the room to the window. It was not yet dark, in fact the sun was setting in a blaze of crimson and orange glory.

Lilian Malvern closed the shutters, and now the light came only from the two tapers burning on either side of a silver mirror. They illuminated the room with a soft glow. There was the fragrance of tiger lilies from two great vases of them. It was an exotic perfume but one which Lilian Malvern loved.

She went softly from the room closing the door behind her. There were tiger lilies in the sitting-room as well but they were accompanied by another flower — the passionate and exotic tuberoses. Lilian Malvern looked around her with the eyes of a producer at the playhouse.

'There are too many lights,' she said to the maid servant. 'Dim three of them.'

It was done; and now she commanded:

'Go to your own quarters and do not come back. Send Jules to me.'

'That will leave no one on the door, m'Lady.'

'It does not matter. If people knock, it will remain unanswered. Besides, Jules will not be long. You have heard what I say. Stay in your own quarters and do not come nosing around until I have need of you.'

'Very good, m'Lady.'

She had almost gone before Lady Malvern shouted out after her:

'And remember, you fool, to see that my chocolate is hot tomorrow morning or I swear that I will throw it at you.'

Into the flunkey's hand she gave the note that she had written earlier in the evening.

'Take it at once to Sir Hengist Wake,' she said. 'If there are other gentlemen with him, draw him to one side by saying it is of the utmost urgency. If, by any chance, he enquires from you how I am, say I am deeply distressed, do you understand?'

'Yes, m'Lady.'

'Now do exactly as I have told you and after you have done that come back here to let Sir Hengist into the apartment. Afterwards you can have the evening off. Go to the tavern or whatever low place you fancy. Keep away, do you understand?'

'Yes, m'Lady.'

'Then hurry. If you linger by the way I will have you flogged.'

Jules was gone before the end of her sentence and Lilian Malvern, with a smile, arranged herself on a low couch covered with cushions. The soft drapery of her negligée fell away from her rounded limbs and her pointed breasts. She rested her head upon a cushion and lay waiting.

It was fifteen minutes later when the door opened abruptly and Sir Hengist came in. She saw at one glance that he was irritated. There was a frown between his eyes and the set of his jaw was grim.

'You wanted me?' he began.

Lilian Malvern gave a little cry and, raising herself from the couch, ran across the room to fling her arms around him.

'Thank God you have come!' she said dramatically. 'Oh, thank you! Thank you! I was so afraid and alone.'

Almost instinctively his arms went round her.

'What is the matter?' he asked. 'What has occurred?'

'I must ask your advice. You must help me,' Lilian Malvern said pulling him towards the couch. 'Sit down so that I may talk with you. Oh, Hengist, I have been off my head with anxiety and fear ever since I heard the news.'

'What news?' he asked.

'I asked myself who could help me,' Lilian Malvern went on without replying to his question, 'and I knew there was only one person whom I could trust.'

'Naturally I will help you,' Sir Hengist said.

'I knew it,' she answered. 'I knew I could rely on you. Hengist! Hengist! How wonderful you are! How good it is to know that I have one real friend in the world.'

She laid her head against his shoulder and wept softly. Her naked shoulders were heaving with emotion; the perfume of her dark, silky hair was in his nostrils. Her hands, desperate in their anxiety, were reaching out to encircle his neck.

'What is it, Lilian? Explain to me,' he said soothingly.

'I was not certain that you would come,' she told him tearfully. 'You do not know what it is like to be a woman and completely alone, to have no man on whom one can rely, to feel miserable and unwanted.'

'I cannot believe you could ever feel that,' Sir Hengist said with a sudden dry note in his voice.

Feeling that she had overdone the dramatics, Lilian Malvern raised her face from his shoulder so that in the soft light he could see how beautiful she was.

'Thank you, dear Hengist,' she said. 'I . . . I feel better, a little less insecure.'

She moved closer to him. He looked down at her gown in surprise. As if she was embarrassed by his glance, Lilian Malvern said quickly:

'Oh, forgive me if I am not properly robed to receive you. I was resting when the news came and I never gave myself a thought. I just remained as I was. All I wanted was your help, your strength.'

'You have not yet told me what is wrong,' Sir Hengist answered.

Her lips were close to his, so close that she felt it would be impossible for him not to kiss her. And yet he made no move to do so.

'I am distraught,' she moaned, 'and find it difficult to put my sentences together, to tell you what has occurred.'

'I cannot help you until I know what it is all about,' Sir Hengist told her.

'It is such a comfort to know that you are here,' she murmured.

She laid her head for a moment longer against his shoulder, and then rose to her feet, knowing that he could not fail to appreciate the sudden glimpse of her legs as the negligée almost fell apart and the pointed perfection of her breasts barely veiled by the transparency of delicate lace.

'Now, where did I put the letter?' she said in distraught tones, putting her long fingers to her temples. 'A groom brought it when I was just about to change my gown. Why, of course, it will be in my bedchamber. Come with me, Hengist. Come and help me find it, for I swear if I see it again I shall swoon, as I have already swooned, with the horror of what it contains.'

'You are making me curious, Lilian,' Sir Hengist said. She knew his eyes were on her and she thought his voice had deepened a little as he watched her movements.

'Come, then,' she begged. 'Please come with me.'

She held out her hands in a beguiling fashion to assist him to arise. As he did so she moved towards him and for a moment it was impossible for him not to hold her. She stood close against him, steadying him with her arms, her lips only a few inches from his.

'I do not know what this is all about, Lilian,' he said. 'Cannot you be a little more explicit? You drag me away from an important audience at which I was particularly asked to be present.'

'No, no, do not think of it,' Lilian Malvern pleaded, her fingers going up to touch his mouth. 'Do not think of anyone but me, I beg you. I am your oldest friend here, someone whom you knew long before you became involved with all these important dignitaries. And, what is more, I am a woman, Hengist, and I need you. I need you

212

desperately. I cannot believe you will fail me.'

Her fingers moved like a caress from his lips to his cheek so that he could answer her.

'You know I will help you in every way I can,' he said. 'I have not forgotten, Lilian, how lovely and tantalising you were when we first met.'

'Have I altered so very much?' she asked in a voice barely above a whisper.

'No,' he answered. 'But . . .'

She knew she must not listen to his excuses. If she was to succeed she must sweep him along on the full tide of her desire.

'There is no time for words,' she told him, scarcely above a whisper. 'Come, let me show you what is worrying me, what has frightened me so terribly. Let me show you the letter which has dashed all my hopes to the ground, which has made me feel that every man's hand is against me and I am all too frail and too weak to fight by myself.'

'Whom is it from?' Sir Hengist asked.

'That I will explain to you once the letter is in your hand,' Lilian Malvern replied. 'But first we must find it. Come with me, Hengist, for I cannot bear to be alone.'

She drew him beguilingly across the room and with her hand still in his, opened the door and led him across the passage. The door of her bedchamber was closed. She opened it and the fragrance of the lilies swept out to greet them and she saw how soft and seductive the room looked in the light of the two tapers.

She led him further into the room and turned towards the great four-poster. Now he would understand, she thought. Now there would be no further need for words.

'Hengist!' she said softly, her lips parted. 'Hengist!' And then her voice rose to a sudden shriek, a cry of sheer terror which rang out round the room, seeming to echo and in echo from the walls, for hanging from the canopy of her bed, his face contorted by the rope which encircled his throat, was Julian Kirk!

9

Andora tossed and turned all night. It seemed to her that a voice at her bedside said accusingly, over and over again:

'You love him! You love him!'

'It was a lie,' she wanted to cry out defiantly; but instead, with a feeling of utter despair, she knew it was the truth.

How could it have happened to her? she asked herself. How could her hate have turned into love? And yet, now she wondered if she ever had really hated Sir Hengist. Had he not merely stung her pride and made her feel piqued because he had laughed and mocked her since the very first moment of her arrival at the Palace?

Restlessly she rose from her bed to go to the window in search of air. And yet she could not be free of him. The ghosts of her memories haunted her whatever she did. She could remember all too vividly how he had come from the gardens into the courtyard below and swept her what she had thought was a mocking bow.

'Sleep well, Andora,' he had called.

She had been incensed with him, but now she thought that her anger had been all pretence and that really she had been glad because he paid her so much attention.

'I cannot understand. It is all too tangled — in my heart, my brain, my pride,' Andora whispered to herself miserably. And yet she knew that only one thing was certain — her love had flamed into life from the very moment that his lips touched hers.

She had known then that all Mary Howard had described so vividly was true, and so much more besides. That sudden breathlessness within her throat, the throbbing within her heart, the feeling as if he had taken possession not only of her lips but of her body. And then that leaping fire searing its way upwards while she felt every nerve of her body quiver with an ecstasy beyond words. It seemed to burn her, to consume her. At the same time she felt small and frail and dependent on the strength of his arms, on the security of his shoulder.

'It is mad, mad, mad!' Andora raged, turning from the window to throw herself down on her bed and hide her burning cheeks in the pillow.

And yet she knew this was love. This was something which could not be denied, something stronger and more tempestuous than anything she had ever encountered in the whole of her sheltered, quiet life.

She had always imagined that love was quiet and peaceful, the drawing together of two people who were attracted by each other into a tender companionship. She had not for a moment guessed that love was like a storm sweeping those who encountered it off their feet and leaving them breathless, buffeted and tormented by the strength and the grandeur if it.

'He has conquered me. I am his prisoner and his slave as completely as if I were a Spaniard whom he has captured in battle,' Andora thought, and wondered how she could even face him again. For one thing was certain — she must never, under any circumstances, let him know.

She thought then that if he guessed that she was attracted to him she would die of the humiliation of it. For he despised her. Had he not said so? Had he not berated her and called her cheap? Had he not poured scorn upon her and kissed her, not because he desired to do so but as a punishment, because he believed that she would hate it above all else?

Andora rolled over on her back, stared up at the ceiling, and thought that never had she known such torture as the conflicting issues within her heart. She knew then that she must go home. She could no longer stay in London when day after day she must see Sir Hengist, knowing what he felt about her.

'Service is above self.'

She started as if she heard her father's voice in the room saying the words; and now she remembered how she had vowed herself to the service of the Queen, to find the traitors who surrounded her. This was more important than her own petty feelings and emotions. Loyalty, in her father's eyes, should supercede everything — even love.

She sat up and bowed her head in her hands; and now, at last, the tears trickled from her eyes and down her cheeks. There was no escape. She had to face him and know that she loved him, whatever he might feel about her.

'Oh, God, why did it have to happen this way?' Andora asked. 'It would have been so easy if I could have loved Lord Murton.'

She wondered why she could not. Why, when he had kissed her, had she felt nothing save a vague distaste and a pity because she could not feel kinder towards him?

All night she lay, feeling, thinking and suffering, and only when the dawn came did she fall into a fitful sleep, to awaken an hour later with a sudden cry on her lips. She heard the sound of it and wondered what she had said and if in her unconsciousness she had committed an indiscretion.

But Grace's smile was reassuring.

'Did I startle you, Mistress?' she enquired. 'I am sorry if I am noisy this morning. It is unusual for you to cry out when I enter the room.'

'I was dreaming,' Andora explained.

' 'Tis a good thing that some people can sleep peaceful,' Grace said cryptically, 'for there be others who've passed a very restless night.'

Andora repressed an impulse to say she was one of them. She knew only too well that Grace wanted to gossip. Although she always decried those who chattered and talked of the scandal in the Palace, there was little that seemed to escape Grace's disapproving ears and she was always ready to relate what she had heard to anyone who would listen.

She drew back the curtains with a little bang and set a cup of chocolate down beside Andora's bed.

'And who has been restless this night?' Andora asked weakly, knowing that it was expected of her and that Grace was but waiting for the question.

'Milady Malvern for one,' Grace said. 'I had it from her own maid that she has been falling into swoon after swoon ever since she found what she found in her bedchamber.'

'And what did she find?' Andora enquired.

Grace paused so that her answer might be fully dramatic.

'The dead body of Master Julian Kirk,' she said at length. 'Hanging by his neck he was, from the canopy of her Ladyship's bed.'

'Grace, it cannot be true! What a terrible thing to have happened! Who is Master Kirk?'

'A young man her Ladyship had enticed with her wiles and her wickedness,' Grace answered. 'She will pay for this when she comes before her Maker, you can be certain of that, Mistress.'

'I should think she will pay long before that,' Andora said practically. 'What will the Queen say?'

'Her Majesty will know naught about it,' Grace replied sharply. 'And do not you go speaking of it either, Mistress. I'm only telling you what I heard in secret from her Ladyship's maid — and she only told me because I am a close friend of hers, seeing that we come from the same village.'

'I had no idea of that,' Andora said. 'Poor Lady Malvern! Cannot one help her in any way?'

'You have no need to involve yourself in evils of that sort,' Grace said. 'Besides, Sir Hengist has seen to everything — even to spiriting the body out of the Palace so no one should know of it.'

Andora was suddenly very still.

'Sir Hengist!' she said.

She could see Lady Malvern coming towards them through the garden, her hands outstretched, her beautiful face alight with pleasure at the sight of Sir Hengist.

'Aye, Sir Hengist,' Grace was saying. 'He was with her Ladyship when she found Master Kirk.'

'He was in Lady Malvern's bedchamber?' Andora asked in a very small voice.

'He was, indeed,' Grace answered with relish. 'And Alice — that is her Ladyship's maid — was told to keep to her own quarters and not to come back until the morning. And the flunkey was told to go to the taverns and enjoy himself. Yes, her Ladyship wanted to be alone with Sir Hengist last night. She did not count on Master Kirk also being present.'

'I do not think I understand,' Andora said. She managed to speak firmly, but her hands were trembling as she drew the bed-clothes a little closer to her as if she was feeling the cold.

' 'Tis clear enough,' Grace answered. 'I warned you, Mistress, of the wicked goings on there are in the Palace. Milady Malvern is an evil woman. Alice told me how, before her poor husband was dead and also when he had hardly been in his coffin a few hours, she was misconducting herself with this Master Julian Kirk — and any other man into whom she could get her claws.'

'I do not think Alice should speak about her mistress in such a way,' Andora managed to say faintly.

'Alice has served her faithfully and well,' Grace said fiercely. 'There was naught else she could do when her family are dependent upon her Ladyship for their house and their livelihood. One word and she would put them all in the gutter — as she has put many others who have offended her on the estate or in the village.'

Andora said nothing. She was still seeing that beautiful face and hearing the sound of that tinkling, musical laughter. She could remember her own shame and humiliation as she had clutched at her torn gown and been conscious of her bruised mouth and untidy hair. She tried to prevent herself from uttering the words and yet the question which was in her mind somehow had to be spoken.

'Does . . . does Sir Hengist love Lady Malvern?'

'Love!' Grace ejaculated contemptuously. 'Her Ladyship does not know the meaning of the word. But she lusts after him, just as she has lusted after other men. Does not the Good Book speak of such people as being in danger of hell fire?'

'Yes, I am sure it does,' Andora said weakly.

'Then judgment will await her Ladyship,' Grace announced. 'Alice says that she sent a note to Sir Hengist after she had dressed herself up in a gown which Jezebel herself might have worn. 'Twas shameless revealing her nakedness; and the room was scented, the wines prepared on the table and most of the tapers blown out.'

Andora shut her eyes in a sudden agony. She could see the scene only too well and Lady Malvern's white hands going out towards Sir Hengist when he came into the room.

'Yes, she had it all planned,' Grace continued. 'But the devil had a surprise for her in the shape of poor Master Kirk. When they went together into the bedchamber, there he was with his neck stretched and his dead eyes almost protruding out of his face.'

'Do not say such things, Grace, be quiet!' Andora cried in a sudden frenzy.

'Sir Hengist had to fetch Alice,' Grace went on unheedingly, 'and she had to go in search of the manservant and fetch him back from the tavern. He and Sir Hengist carried Master Kirk's body down one of the side staircases so that no one should know where he had died or what had happened.'

'If the servants talk, everyone will learn of it,' Andora said quickly.

'The flunkey will tell no one,' Grace said. 'For Sir Hengist has given him several gold pieces and her Ladyship has sent him back to the country this very morning.'

'And what about her maid Alice?' Andora enquired.

'Sir Hengist gave her a gold piece as well,' Grace said enviously. ' "I know you are a good girl," he said. "Look after your mistress and keep your mouth shut, for if anyone should hear of what has happened this night it could do her great damage." '

'But Alice has told you,' Andora said accusingly.

'That is different,' Grace replied laconically. 'I am like a sister to her and I shall be telling no one but you, Mistress, you can be sure of that. 'Tis only that I wish to warn you of the devil's own doings that take place in this Palace.'

'I would rather not hear of them,' Andora answered.

She wished she could feel more sorry for Lady Malvern. Instead, she knew that she was consumed by a jealousy which made her close her eyes with the very pain of it.

Sir Hengist had gone to Lady Malvern's apartments. He had kissed her and made love to her in her shameless, revealing robe before they had gone into the bedchamber. She could see that red, passionate mouth upheld to his. She could see the dark, lustrous hair dressed with jewels thrown back or resting against his shoulder, the way her head had rested earlier in the day.

'If this is love,' she thought to herself — and she felt faint at the intensity of her suffering — 'then Heaven grant me that I may only hate.'

Later in the morning the Queen, whose sharp eyes missed nothing, exclaimed at her pallor.

'What ails you, child? Are you sickening for some putrid fever?' she enquired.

Andora shook her head.

'It is nothing, Your Majesty. I have a slight headache.'

'I swear this Palace is damp,' the Queen said. 'The walls are thick and the floors strong, but the mists of night gather beneath our windows and that, I swear, is bad for us all.'

'Yet I have never seen Your Majesty look so well,' Mistress Parry remarked.

'It is true, I feel well,' the Queen replied. 'I am happy and that is better medicine than any apothecary can concoct.'

She smiled at her Maids-of-Honour.

'Remember that,' she told them. 'It is happiness that makes a woman seem young and beautiful. Happiness because she knows that she has the power to love and be loved.'

A little later the Queen wrote her habitual note to Lord Essex and tossed it in the air towards Andora.

'Run along, my little country mouse,' she said. 'The fresh air may bring some roses to your cheeks.'

Andora had planned that she would protest and ask if someone could go in her stead. But now that the moment was upon her she had not the courage, and catching the note she went from the room and hurried down the passage, feeling that if she did not go with haste she would not be brave enough to go at all.

And yet, as she drew nearer to the sundial where she was wont to meet Sir Hengist, she knew suddenly that all the time she had been longing for this moment. Beneath her fears and beneath her reluctance she wanted, above all things, to see him.

Perhaps it was enough to know that he was alive and well and that his very existence in the world justified her love of him. Even her jealousy and her unhappiness seemed to pale beside the fact that she was to see him again; and even if he despised her, it was better than if he felt no emotion towards her at all.

He appeared suddenly, striding along the flagged path and making the garden seem smaller and less important because he himself was so big and so magnificent in his embroidered doublet.

Andora felt herself tremble as she waited for him to come towards her. And then, because she could not bear to look up into his face, her long eyelashes swept her cheeks as she curtsied and shyly held out the Queen's note.

'Thank you, Andora. Her Majesty is well, I trust?'

'Her Majesty is well and in excellent spirits.'

'Good! Tell her my Lord Essex enquired

particularly as to her health.'

'I will relate what you have told me,' Andora said, her voice barely above a whisper.

She realised now that Sir Hengist had been talking to her in a strictly conventional tone. His voice was courteous, but without warmth. She felt almost as if he put a steel curtain around himself, a barrier which she could not penetrate. He handed her a note from Lord Essex.

'Kindly convey this to Her Majesty,' he said, and again his tone was strictly formal and she felt his impatience and the fact that he was about to turn and leave her.

She opened her eyes because she felt she must look at him and found him staring down at her as if suddenly arrested by something she had seen.

'You look pale, Andora,' he said in a very different tone of voice, 'and there are dark lines under your eyes. You are not ill?'

'No, I . . . I have a headache, that is all,' Andora replied.

'You are quite certain it is nothing more serious? The nights can often be treacherous at this time of year. If you have caught a chill and you feel there are any signs of the fever upon you, you must go at once to Her Majesty's physician.'

'I . . . am quite all right,' Andora persisted.

'It is not like you to seem so listless . . .' he began with unexpected kindness.

The change in his voice brought the tears welling up into Andora's eyes and to her horror and consternation she felt as if she was going to burst into sobs. His indifference to her was easier to bear when he was harsh, but when he was kind it made her unhappiness all too intense.

In a wild effort to control her tears she dropped him a little curtsy.

'I . . . I must go, my . . . Lord,' she stammered, and to her horror her voice broke on the last word. She turned to run from the garden, but he was too quick for her and reaching out caught her hand in his.

'Andora,' he said. 'What has happened? It cannot be what I said or did to you yesterday, for I promise you . . .'

'Let me go! Let me go!' she said wildly.

She dragged her hand from his.

'Have you . . . not done . . . enough?' she asked; and now the tears streaming down her face were making her completely incoherent.

It was impossible to say any more. She could only pick up her skirts and run away from him as swiftly as she could towards the shelter of the Palace. When she reached the sanctuary of the door to the Queen's apartments, she stood for a moment fighting for self-control. Then she mopped up her tears and on entering the room handed the note to Elizabeth, who opened it quickly without a glance towards the messenger who had brought it.

As soon as she dared, Andora asked Mistress Parry for permission to retire and reaching her own bedchamber she washed her face in cold water and took herself severely to task for being so weak and childish. What must he think of her? she thought, struggling with him like that and running away when he was but being considerate as regards her health.

Supposing he thought that she was afraid that he might kiss her again? Her face burned at the thought. How foolish she must have appeared to him! He was used to sophisticated ladies of the Court who would kiss and flirt in the evening and on the following day forget the very name of the man they had favoured.

Why could she not behave in a more worldly manner instead of like a simpleton from some country village? Andora scolded herself and then went back to her duties, aware now that the falsehood of the morning had become the truth of the afternoon for her head throbbed intolerably.

The Maids-of-Honour had arranged a game of battledore and shuttlecock in the gardens that afternoon, but Andora managed to make her excuses. She wandered upstairs to where she found Mistress Parry poring over her fortune-telling cards in a corner of the sitting-room.

'Do you want me to tell your fortune, dear?' she asked.

Andora shook her head. She knew only too well that her future held heartbreak and longing for a man who had no interest in her save to find her tiresome and irresponsible, and loneliness because without him life seemed empty and pointless.

'What I want of the future,' she told herself, 'is a husband and children and a house in the country where I can be quiet and happy and forget all the intrigues and the scheming that surrounds those who live in proximity to the Queen.'

It was impossible not to think of Sir Hengist and the manservant carrying the dead body of Julian Kirk down one of the small, twisting passages which led to the garden. Then they would have slipped like ghosts outside the Palace wall and somehow rid themselves of the corpse in a manner which would never have brought suspicion upon themselves.

They may have thrown him in a ditch or placed him in an alley-way where he would have been found next morning or as likely as not they had dumped him in the river so that he would have been carried out to sea by the tide.

Andora shook herself and tried to make her thoughts turn in another direction. But it was hard to concentrate on anything else except Sir Hengist and the beauty of Lady Malvern. Yet after a time the peace and the quietness of the room and the scent of the roses coming through the windows made her relax a little. Some of the tension went from her and the throbbing of her head eased.

She sank back against the cushions in the chair, watching Mistress Parry turn over the cards, and tried to tell herself that the horror of what she had heard and the stupidity of her behaviour in the garden would pass, as everything else passed in time.

She must have slept a little, for she awoke with a start to find that the sun had moved from the window and now a faint wind was rustling her hair. The door opened suddenly; a page looked in and coming across to Andora's side said in a whisper:

'Mistress Andora Bland?'

'Yes,' Andora answered a little sleepily, and then sat up quickly. 'Does the Queen have need of me?'

'No, not the Queen,' the page replied, still in a whisper so that Mistress Parry could not hear. 'But there is someone who wishes to see you at the eastern door of the Palace.'

'To see me!' Andora said in surprise. 'Who is it?'

'Someone who comes from your home and has a message for you,' the page answered.

'If it is someone from my home, invite him to come up here,' Andora said.

The page glanced over his shoulder towards Mistress Parry.

'That is not possible.'

'Then ask him to send me his name,' Andora said.

She looked at the page's livery and realised that she did not recognise it.

'Who is your master?' she enquired.

The page shook his head and went from the room, leaving Andora perturbed and a little worried. If anyone had really come to see her from her home, she thought, they had but to ask at the main door of the Palace and they would be escorted to the Maids-of-Honours' apartments.

She had a sudden feeling that this was one

of Lord Murton's schemes to see her alone. And yet the page had not worn his livery. Anyway, she had no intention of going down to the eastern gate unattended or without permission. It was the kind of thing the Queen would consider most reprehensible on the part of one of her Maids-of-Honour.

It must have been Lord Murton, she thought. She shut her eyes and tried to go to sleep again, but not for long. The Maids-of-Honour came back, chattering and laughing about their game of battledore and shuttle-cock, telling Andora how the Queen had joined in and played better than any of them.

'There is nothing that she cannot do better than us,' Elizabeth Trentham said with a sigh. 'It is really very depressing.'

'She is old,' Lady Mary Howard replied. 'You know as well as I do that she would give half her kingdom to be young again, to be the same age as my Lord Essex.'

'Oh, do be careful, Mary,' Elizabeth Trentham said. 'You will be confined to your room again — or, worse still, sent to the Tower — if you keep saying such things of the Queen. I know someone will overhear you one day and report it.'

'Did you see the way Lady Malvern was

behaving this afternoon?' A pretty red-headed Maid-of-Honour enquired in an effort to change the subject. 'She was making such a fuss of Her Majesty that I thought her flattery and her compliments must sound insincere — even to someone as partial to such things as the Queen. But, no, she seemed to enjoy every word of it and invited Lady Malvern to dine with her tonight.'

'Personally I cannot bear her,' Elizabeth Trentham said in a surprisingly firm voice, for she was usually so reticent about expressing her feelings. 'There is something about Lady Malvern which makes me creep and yet I cannot think what it is.'

'I could tell her,' Andora thought, but instead she kept silent until Mary Howard said affectionately:

'Are you better, Andora? We missed you this afternoon and the Queen was quite perturbed to hear that you still felt poorly. "What shall I do without my messenger of love?" she said.'

'Her Majesty honours me,' Andora answered.

'And she finds you useful,' Elizabeth Trentham remarked. 'She would not dare to send Mary to carry her messages for fear of what she would be up to on the journeys

— and that goes for Bridget and a great number of the others.'

The girl of whom she spoke pretended to be incensed and picking up the cushions out of a chair began to throw them at Elizabeth. In the midst of the tumult Andora escaped to her own bedchamber.

There was nothing to do now, she thought, until dinner time and she sat down to write a letter to her father, wondering how she could put into conventional words the ordinary activities of the Court and not reveal to him the chaos and tumult of her own thoughts and feelings.

She had only just begun the letter when there was a knock at the door.

'Come in,' Andora called, and the door opened to reveal not Grace, as she had expected, but a strange maid whom she had never seen before.

'What is it?' Andora asked.

'I am Alice, if it please you, Mistress Bland, maid to Milady Malvern.'

'Oh, I have heard Grace speak of you,' Andora said with a smile. 'She tells me that you come from the same village.'

'We do, indeed, Mistress. And Milady Malvern has sent me to say that she wishes to have a word with you.'

Andora felt herself start at the suggestion

and a feeling of distaste and disgust made her long to refuse instantly. But politeness made her ask:

'Where is her Ladyship?'

'Just outside,' Alice replied. 'She sent me to speak with you for she did not wish to come herself if you were not alone.'

'I do not understand,' Andora said, bewildered.

'Let me explain,' a melodious voice interrupted, and Lady Malvern suddenly swept into the room, her gown of red satin shining in the smiling sun, the jewels round her neck and in her hair sparkling as if to accentuate her radiance. Combined with the fragrance of an exotic perfume she wore it all seemed to Andora to be very overpowering.

She rose quickly from the desk at which she was writing and curtsied. As she did so she felt a sudden revulsion against this woman whose secret she knew and whom she both mistrusted and disliked.

'Mistress Bland, you must forgive me coming to you like this and in such a strange manner,' Lady Malvern said ingratiatingly. 'But I beg you to come with me at once on an errand of mercy.'

'To come with you, Madam!' Andora exclaimed. 'But why?'

'There is someone waiting outside who is

desperately anxious to see you,' Lady Malvern replied.

'A page has already informed me of that,' Andora answered. 'But if it is anyone who wishes to see me, they have but to ask permission and then can be brought to these apartments.'

'It is not as easy as that,' Lady Malvern said. 'Do you remember Ned Fowler?'

'The forester's son who was sent to prison for poaching?' Andora asked. 'Of course I do.'

'He is outside,' Lady Malvern told her. 'But in trying to escape his captors he has injured his leg and therefore cannot come to you, even if he dared to do so.'

'He has escaped!' Andora cried. 'But how dare he come here?'

'He is with his mother,' Lady Malvern said, 'and they wish you to take a petition to Her Majesty on their behalf.'

'Oh, poor Ned! I always thought he was wrongly convicted,' Andora said.

'That is what I have been told,' Lady Malvern replied.

'I know a lot of people thought that Ned got his desserts, but I always believed that he had been wrongly charged,' Andora said eagerly. 'You say that they have come here all this way?'

'Someone who had their interests at heart brought them in a coach,' Lady Malvern answered. 'But there is no time to be lost. Will you not come and speak with poor Ned?'

'Of course I will,' Andora answered.

Lady Malvern looked round the room.

'I should put a cloak over your gown,' she said. 'You do not want people asking questions if they should see you.'

'No, of course not,' Andora replied.

She took her dark travelling cloak from a cupboard. Lady Malvern glanced at her maid who was standing in the background, her eyes lowered, her face expressionless.

'Alice will take you to where the coach is waiting,' Lady Malvern told Andora. 'She knows exactly where it is, do you not, Alice?'

'Yes, m'Lady,' Alice answered, a little glumly Andora thought.

'Then hurry,' Lady Malvern admonished her. 'There is none too much time before Mistress Bland should be on duty again. Hurry! Hurry!'

Following Alice, who went ahead, Andora slipped out of the Maids-of-Honours' apartments and down the passages. She noticed that Alice was leading her by the back ways known perhaps only to the servants and valets in the Palace. They twisted and turned, went down one staircase, along another passage and came out by what Andora guessed was the eastern gate.

Alice had walked so fast that Andora had difficulty in catching up with her, but now they were outside she seemed to slow her footsteps.

'What a lot of ways there are in and out of the Palace!' she said breathlessly to Alice. 'I hope I can find my way back and I must try and find Ned somewhere to hide while I take his petition to the Queen.'

Alice did not answer, and Andora, glancing at her face, thought she looked sour and rather disagreeable. For the first time she wondered why Lady Malvern of all people should know about Ned, a boy from her father's estate.

But there was not time to wonder or to ask questions. The gates were ahead and outside, waiting in the dusty road, Andora could see a coach. The gate was open, the sentries were not interested in anyone leaving the Palace, only in those entering it.

Andora hurried across the road and only as she reached the coach did she realise that Alice had not accompanied her but was waiting behind at the gate. She put out her hand towards the handle of the door and as she did so the door swung open. She bent forward, putting out her hands to steady herself.

'Are you there, Ned?' she asked, for she saw that the curtains were drawn over the windows and it was dark inside.

There was movement and she said again:

'Ned. It is Andora Bland. You remember me, do you not?'

Then two strong hands seized hold of her arms and lifted her up. She felt them pulling her into the coach; and even as she gave a little cry of surprise at their roughness, as she began to say that there was no need for such impetuosity, she felt herself flung roughly on to a seat.

The coach door slammed behind her and before she could recover her senses or even realise what was happening, she felt the coachman whip up the horses and the coach started off.

10

For a moment Andora could only gasp with fear and then she managed to find her voice and cried:

'What is happening? Who are you? Where are you taking me?'

In answer a hand reached out and drew back the curtains which covered the windows of the coach. The light came flooding in and she saw, to her astonishment, that she was seated next to an elegant, rather raffish young man in a resplendent doublet and plumed hat, while opposite him sat another gallant equally well dressed.

'Stop this coach at once!' Andora cried as she realised that the horses were gathering speed.

'I am afraid, Mistress Bland, that is impossible,' the gentleman seated next to her said. His voice was cultured and his smile disarming as he added: 'for the purposes of this journey may I introduce myself as Gilbert? My friend opposite is known as Charles.'

'For the purposes of what journey?' Andora enquired. 'How dare you carry me off in this manner? And where are you taking me?'

'That is not to be revealed,' the gentleman called Charles replied. 'But I think your heart may tell you the answer.'

'My heart?' Andora asked in puzzled tones. 'What do you mean by that?'

As she spoke she glanced out of the window and realised that they were already out in the countryside, travelling at a speed which made the coach rock from side to side and forced her to balance herself carefully if she were not to be flung into the stranger's arms.

'We are taking you to someone who loves you,' Gilbert said. 'Is not that so, Charles?'

'It is, in fact, a very exciting adventure,' the young man opposite Andora drawled.

'But I have no wish to be involved in any adventure,' Andora cried. 'You tricked and deceived me. I was told by Lady Malvern that Ned was here — a boy from my village who had been taken to prison for poaching.'

'I expect some story had to be concocted to lure you away from the sacred precincts of Her Majesty's apartments!' Charles replied with a little twist of his lips.

'The Queen will certainly be angry when

she hears of this escapade,' Andora said.

'We shall have to think of some good explanation to give her,' Charles answered soothingly.

'I shall tell Her Majesty the truth, you can be quite certain of that,' Andora retorted. 'It will go hard with you who have been a party to what it seems to me is nothing but a kidnapping.'

'I see that we shall have to throw ourselves on your mercy,' Charles smiled. 'To tell the truth, Mistress Bland, we are but doing a good turn to a friend of ours.'

'And who is that?' Andora asked.

'You will learn his name in good time,' Charles replied quickly. 'All we have been asked to do is to bring you to where he is waiting eagerly — with outstretched arms.'

'I think you are mad or crazed,' Andora said sharply. 'Let me make this quite clear. I have no desire to meet any gentleman — whoever he may be — in this clandestine and ridiculous manner. If it is a joke, then it has gone far enough. If it is a serious attempt to carry me away from the Palace, then I promise you the Queen shall hear of it.'

She saw the two men glance at each other, but she could not determine what message they conveyed wordlessly to one another.

She looked through the window again and saw the country was getting wilder and she guessed that they were travelling by an un-frequented road, for there were few people to be seen and only an occasional cottage or shack.

'Can I beg of you to stop this farce?' she said, changing her tone. 'I assure you, gen-tlemen, that whoever instigated this absurd idea of capturing me and carrying me away must, in fact, be my worst enemy. If it is some prank, then I shall get into a great deal of trouble — in fact, I may even be dis-missed from my post. The Queen has no liking for such behaviour in one of her Maids-of-Honour.'

She saw the gentlemen glance at each other once again and became convinced that this was, in fact, some joke. At first she had been afraid and had suspected some-thing sinister and unpleasant; but the two men were obviously gentlemen of substance and they looked too young and irrespon-sible to be engaged in any intrigue or polit-ical activity.

She had heard tell since she had been at Court of all sorts of instances when jokes had been played on the Maids-of-Honour and rather boisterous ragging was, she knew, often indulged in by the younger gentlemen of the Court.

'I beg you, gentlemen,' she said again, 'to turn the coach round and let us go back. You have had your fun; you have deceived me into believing that I was going to succour a man who had escaped from Her Majesty's prison. That would be hard enough to explain in itself. If I am late in attendance upon the Queen in the Great Hall tonight, there will be enquiries as to what has happened to me and I cannot help but involve you both.'

'Only unfortunately you do not know who we are,' Charles said, a note of glee in his voice.

'You will not be hard to trace,' Andora told him. 'And, what is more, I have a good memory for faces.'

'In which case, of course, we shall have to dispose of you before you can tell tales about us,' Gilbert suggested lightly.

Andora smiled. She was angry, but he was so ridiculous.

'That would be an easy solution, would it not?' she asked. 'Unfortunately, a Queen's Maid-of-Honour found with her throat cut would cause quite a stir. Her Majesty might even send the Military to make enquiries as to what had happened.'

Charles laughed.

'I see that you have to remain alive,' he said. 'But we have given our word of honour to hand you over to the gentleman who so earnestly seeks your company. You would not expect us to break a solemn oath, would you?'

'I expect you to show a little bit of good sense,' Andora said crossly. 'This is all very childish and irresponsible. Turn the coach round and let us stop talking of this nonsensical scheme which can only bring trouble and maybe punishment on those engaged in it.'

'We cannot. I promise you we cannot,' Gilbert said. 'I am sorry we cannot oblige you, Mistress Bland. You are prettier, far prettier, than we imagined from the description of you.'

'I am flattered,' Andora answered sarcastically. 'But flattery does not make me any less incensed with what is occurring. We must have been travelling for over half an hour. How much farther have we got to go? Her Majesty will be expecting me to be in attendance within the hour.'

'It is not very much farther now,' Gilbert replied, looking through the window.

Andora looked out too. The land was flat and from the glimpse of silver she caught now and again she guessed that they were still beside the river. From the position of the sun she realised that they were going east and she thought, with a kind of despair, that this was the sort of escapade which would make the Queen very angry.

How could she explain that she had no part in it? That she knew nothing about it? No one was going to believe her. And what was more, the Queen, who was very harsh on her Maids-of-Honours' flirtations, would be sure to think that she had encouraged whichever gentleman was involved in this piece of stupidity.

'Oh, please, please,' Andora said in desperation, 'do cease this foolishness and let me go back. It is all so stupid and idiotic and will amuse nobody — not even yourselves — when retribution comes, which it is bound to do.'

'I am sorry,' Gilbert said, 'but there is, indeed, nothing we can do about it.'

Now he was not smiling and for a moment Andora felt a little tremor of fear. Was there really something more sinister behind this mad chase into the empty countryside than the light-hearted mischief of some stupid young gallants about the Court?

She tried to remember if she had ever seen either Gilbert or Charles before and decided that their faces were unfamiliar. And yet it was difficult to be sure. She had been such a short time in the Palace and the gallants all appeared to look alike in their small, silken beards and colourful doublets.

What a fool she had been to believe the story Lady Malvern had told her! Why had she not stopped to consider that it would be most unlikely that Lady Malvern would know of Ned or anyone else from her village. Instead, like a simple country bumpkin, she had believed everything she was told and had gone rushing to the gate without even asking questions.

With a sense of frustration that made her want to scream with exasperation Andora realised that the miles were slipping away beneath the horses' hoofs, carrying her farther and farther from the Palace and her duty.

Charles suddenly bent forward to peer out of the window, then said:

'Best draw the curtains.'

'What for?' Andora asked as their hands reached up to draw the heavy, dark material across the windows.

'We will explain in a moment,' Gilbert said cheerfully. 'And now we must ask you, Mistress Bland, to allow us to bandage your eyes.'

'This is getting more ridiculous every moment,' Andora expostulated. 'I shall allow you to do nothing of the sort.'

'If you refuse, I am afraid we shall have to use force,' he replied.

He spoke quietly, but somehow she sensed a hint of steel beneath his words which made her feel again that sudden stab of fear.

'Is . . . is this part of the game?' she asked uneasily.

'It is, indeed,' he answered. 'And we must beg of you not to struggle or make a fuss, because having gone so far the game has to be played out to the very end.'

Andora swallowed a little nervously. Now the coach was darkened and she could barely see the outline of the two men sitting with her. She began to feel that, after all, this was no light-hearted prank. There was something in Gilbert's voice which made her wary and on her guard.

Was this the danger that Sir Hengist had warned her about? Mentally she shook herself. It was absurd to think that these two overdressed popinjays could in any way be connected with a Spanish plot against the Queen. No, they were only ordinary young men such as might be seen at any time hanging around the Court. All the same, she knew that her hands were trembling a little as Charles drew a bandage from his pocket and slipped it over her eyes and tied it behind her head.

'Are you quite certain you cannot see?' he asked.

'No, the bandage is too thick,' Andora answered.

'Then do not try to do so,' he said. 'It will be better for you to accept what is happening, and if you should struggle or shout I must warn you that no one will pay any attention and Charles and I might have to be rough with you.'

'Rough with me?' Andora asked. 'Surely you are joking?'

'No, indeed,' he answered. 'We are merely carrying out our instructions to take you where you have to go.'

Andora knew then that a strange fear had been stalking her all through this journey. Now it pounced to grip her so that she bit her lips in a sudden terror lest she should scream and struggle. It would have been ineffective and undignified, she knew. Besides, it would proclaim her cowardice and above all things, as her father's daughter, she must be brave.

She could hear her father talking to her as he had so often done about his battles and the manner in which the men under him had fought.

'Being brave is not being unafraid,' he had said, 'but consists in not showing one's fear. The bravest men can be afraid when faced with overwhelming odds, with death and a superior enemy. But the bravest ones are those who go on fighting and never give in. That is why the English always win in the end, Andora — because they go on fighting.'

'I will not show them I am afraid,' Andora thought now; and suddenly it came to her it would be best for her not to show that she imagined there was anything serious or sinister behind what was happening, but to pretend, as they had pretended at the beginning, that it was all a lighthearted game, a part of some romantic episode in which a lovelorn swain desired her company.

With a tremendous effort she forced a smile to her lips.

'I swear you are beginning to intrigue me,' she said, 'What awaits me at journey's end?'

'That you will soon find out,' Gilbert replied. 'Though you still have a little farther to go.'

The horses were slowing down and a moment later they were brought to a standstill. Gilbert drew back the curtains.

'It is muddy here,' he said, 'and your slippers will be spoilt by the rough ground. If you are wise, you will let me carry you rather than stumble blindly along, not knowing where you are going.'

'I think that is a good idea,' Andora replied, still trying to speak as if she were faintly amused at what was occurring. At the same time it was agony for her to sit there with her eyes bound, knowing that she dared not raise the bandage from her eyes and yet longing with every nerve of her body to know what was happening and where she was going.

She heard Gilbert call out:

'Is everything ready?' and a rough, uneducated voice replied:

'Aye, that it be, Sir.'

He lifted her in his arms and carried her across uneven ground. She could not see, she could but listen, and now she heard the lap of water, the sudden splash of oar. A moment later she was set down in what she knew to be a row-boat. She heard Gilbert say:

'Get into the stern, Charles.'

She heard the other man come aboard. The boat was being pushed off from the side and now the oars were in the water and someone was rowing hard. After a few moments she decided that the boat was bigger than she had thought; there were two men at the oars and they were moving swiftly across the river.

Was she being taken aboard a ship? Andora wondered. And, if so, for what purpose? She longed to ask questions, but she knew that she would get no answer to them and she was afraid that if she spoke more than was absolutely necessary her voice would tremble and they would know how frightened she was.

She thought of her father and wondered if he knew, in the manner in which he did so often know things, that she was in trouble. She thought of the Maids-of-Honour chattering as they got ready to be in attendance on the Queen. Then she thought of Sir Hengist.

It seemed to her in that moment as if her heart winged its way towards him crying for help, begging him to come and save her, as he had saved her once before when he had come unexpectedly into Lord Braye's apartment.

'Save me! Save me!'

She almost said the words aloud, so intense were her feelings. She felt as if her desire for him must reach him wherever he was. But she remembered despairingly how he despised her and, therefore, even if he thought of her it would not be with kindness or even with a desire to help.

Yet somehow even the thought of him, because she loved him, seemed to ease her fear. He had been with Drake. He had fought and killed and lived to return to England, would there be any return for her?

For the first time, it seemed to Andora, the full significance of what was happening began to strike her. She had been captured and carried away from the very Palace itself. It must, therefore, be somebody who needed her very desperately or he would not have undertaken such desperate measures. But for what?

The wind blowing down the river was cold. She pulled her cloak closer about her and shivered. Then with a quick change of mood she told herself it was all ridiculous. This romp had no political significance. She was a supremely unimportant person. Why should anyone bother to capture her? Unless it was, in fact, as Gilbert had said, someone who had lost his heart to her.

There could be only one person whom that description would fit, and yet she could not believe that Lord Murton had a hand in this.

The boat suddenly grated against what Andora guessed was a quay. She knew that the men rowing were standing up and holding the boat steady while Gilbert reached down and picked her up in his arms.

'I will hand her to you, Charles,' he said.

The boat was rocking a little against the tide. Andora found herself passed from one man to another, almost as if she were a parcel.

'Will 'ee be wantin' us again, Sir?' one of the boatmen asked.

'Yes, we are returning with you,' Gilbert replied. Andora felt a quick relief. So they did not intend to remain here long.

Charles did not hold Andora so securely as Gilbert had done although he was walking steadily on what she guessed was a firmly made road. She had a feeling that they were passing over a bridge or a moat and then she heard a heavy door open and a voice ask:

'Is all well?'

'Everything went according to plan,' Gilbert replied.

'She is to come this way,' the voice said.

'Put her down,' Gilbert ordered Charles, 'she can walk now.'

Andora felt herself set down on her feet;

then Gilbert fumbled with the knot of the bandage which bound her eyes, and because he was slow she reached up and removed it herself.

For a moment she thought she had gone blind and then she realised that the place in which she stood was very dark — in fact only after a few seconds did she manage to discern the figures of Gilbert and Charles. As she turned towards them, they moved to the door through which they had all entered and it closed behind them.

In the sudden terror she would have run after them, but the person who had let them in and who she saw now was a sour-faced middle-aged man, said abruptly:

'This way, Mistress!'

It was a command and instinctively Andora followed him.

'Where am I?' Andora asked.

'At the end of your journey,' he replied. 'You have no farther to go.'

'I am glad of that,' she said. 'But what is this place?'

'That is not for me to tell you,' he said. 'Come, they're waiting.'

He led her across what Andora could now see was, in fact, a great arched hall towards a door that was open. There was light shining through it, and now they entered a long room in which were standing three people. One of them stepped forward towards her and Andora saw it was Lord Murton.

'Andora! You are safe!' he exclaimed.

His hands were outstretched, but she made no movement to put her fingers in his.

'I think, my Lord, you owe me an explanation,' she said stiffly.

'There is no time for that,' an elderly man said harshly.

Andora turned to look at him. He was a tall, gaunt looking man with a grey beard and the remains of what must once have been handsome good looks. She could see in him some resemblance to Lord Murton and was not surprised when the latter said in an insistent voice:

'Father, let me handle this my way.'

'There is no time I tell you,' the Earl of Thanet protested.

The third person present spoke now. He was dressed in sombre, drab garments which seemed strangely out of place and ill fitting on him. But he spoke with authority and his deep, resonant, educated voice seemed to command attention.

'I should let the boy do it his way, my Lord.'

'Do what?' Andora asked. 'What is all this about?'

'That is exactly what I want to explain to

you,' Lord Murton said. 'Come with me into another room. We cannot talk with all these people listening.'

His father would have said something again, but the strange man put a hand on his arm and with a shrug of his shoulders he turned away.

Andora drew a deep breath.

'My Lord,' she said. 'I do not know why you have brought me here or what prank it may be; but I assure you that if it is, in fact, a joke, it has gone far enough. I am in attendance on Her Majesty tonight. If I am not there, enquiries will be made and my reputation may suffer because of what has occurred. I pray you, return me immediately to the Palace. And if this is a joke, I promise you, unless I am very seriously reprimanded because of my absence, I will say nothing of what has happened.'

'I am sorry, Andora, but I cannot do that,' Lord Murton said. 'Come with me and I will explain.'

'I . . . I do not understand,' Andora answered, looking from him towards the two other men.

'I know that you do not,' Lord Murton said soothingly. 'That is why I want to explain things to you. Please, Andora, come as I suggest.'

'Very well,' she agreed.

He led the way across the room to where another door led into a smaller apartment. It was more comfortably furnished and Andora realised that the hall had contained no furniture at all and the room in which she had met Lord Murton and his father had only a carpet on the floor and a table and a few scattered chairs in it.

In this smaller room a fire was burning and there were several comfortable chairs drawn up in front of it. There was wine on the table and when Lord Murton poured her out a glass she would have refused it had he not said:

'I should drink a little. What I have to tell you may come as a shock.'

Because she wished to disguise her own fears she took the glass and as she did so walked across the room to look out of the window. Below her she saw a moat and beyond it flat, uncultivated fields stretching away to where the river, wide and molten silver, flowed towards the sea. She could see the road by which she must have travelled ending at a stone jetty on the other side of the river. There was not a house in sight.

'Where are we?' she asked.

'Where no one would ever expect to find you,' Lord Murton replied unexpectedly.

She wheeled round on him.

'What do you mean by that? What are you doing? Why am I here?'

'I brought you here to marry me!'

'Are you mad? Do you suppose that I would marry you under such circumstances? Without the permission of my father; without knowing you better.'

'Andora, you have got to marry me.'

'Got to! I do not know what you are talking about.'

He walked across to her and took her hands in his.

'Try and understand,' he said. 'This is urgent and serious. You have got to marry me now, this moment. There are reasons that I cannot explain, but good reasons, that make it imperative that you should be my wife.'

Andora pulled her hands from his.

'And you think I would marry you when you have treated me like this?' she asked. 'Bringing me here against my will; coercing me from the Palace with lies; bandaging my eyes and talking about urgent reasons which you do not explain. If this is your idea of a proposal, my Lord, your answer is no.'

'But, Andora, you cannot refuse me. We have to be married at once.'

'What, here? In this place?' Andora enquired.

'A priest is waiting,' Lord Murton said.

'A priest!'

Andora repeated the words slowly, her eyes widening. She knew then what had seemed wrong with the man who spoke with authority and yet wore drab clothes which seemed to fit him ill.

He was a priest of the Catholic Church; a fugitive hiding — as so many Catholic priests were forced to hide — in the Castle of some great noble who outwardly expressed allegiance to Elizabeth but whose faith had remained steadfast since the rule of her half-sister. She remembered hearing how the Spanish priests had invaded England secretly, slipping in disguise into all parts of the country to foster the faith and aid Spain.

'Yes, a priest,' Lord Murton said steadily.

'He is not a priest of my faith,' Andora retorted. 'I am a Protestant.'

'And I am a Catholic,' Lord Murton said. 'But such differences can be overcome. Later we will have a dispensation. Now it is urgent that we should be man and wife.'

'Perhaps you could give me a good reason why I should accept you,' Andora suggested.

'I can give you one very good reason,' he replied. 'If you do not marry me you will be in very real danger, Andora.'

'Danger from whom?' Andora enquired.

'From my father and the other men who are here. Oh, Andora, believe me when I tell you that, in truth, I do love you deeply.'

'You have a strange way of showing it, my Lord,' she retorted.

She took a little sip of the wine, then set the glass down on the table. She felt as if her legs would carry her no longer, and she sat down in one of the chairs in front of the fire.

'What do they want of me?' she asked simply.

'You must marry me before you tell them,' Lord Murton said in a low voice. 'Do you not understand that once they know what you have to tell there will be no reason for keeping you alive, unless you are, in fact, my wife?'

Andora gazed at him with startled eyes.

'But what can I know that could be of the least interest to such people?' she asked in surprise.

Lord Murton glanced over his shoulder at the door, then dropping down on his knee beside her chair he whispered against her ear:

'What you overheard in the Queen's

chamber when the Admiral told her where Francis Drake had taken his fleet.'

For a moment the full import of his words did not sink into Andora's brain, and then suddenly she saw it all. She was in possession of a secret which the Spaniards, and those who gave their allegiance to the enemies of England, would give much to know.

Sir Francis Drake, as the Admiral had said, had gone in search of the *San Filipe*, the great carrack which contained the spoils of the East. If Spain could be certain of this, they could not only prevent him from reaching her, they could destroy him and his whole fleet.

Very slowly, to give herself time to think, Andora rose to her feet.

'I should not have suspected you, my Lord,' she said quietly, 'of being a traitor. You have masked your villainy well.'

'Andora, do not trouble your head with such matters,' Lord Murton begged. 'Marry me and all will be well. I will protect you. You will be my wife. Your life will be safe.'

Andora looked at him with a scorn that seemed to blaze in her white face.

'I would not marry you, my Lord,' she declared, 'if you were the last man on earth. I loathe and despise you. I only hope that I shall live long enough to unmask your villainy, so that you may never deceive Her Majesty again.'

'If you talk like that I cannot help you,' Lord Murton said almost despairingly.

'I do not want your help,' Andora stormed at him.

The door opened and the Earl of Thanet came into the room.

'Well? Has she agreed?' he asked in uncompromising tones.

'No, I have not, my Lord,' Andora said. 'I have just told your son that I would not marry him if he were the last man on earth. And I am ashamed that Englishmen such as yourselves should attempt to help the enemies of our country.'

'We are doing our best for England in our way,' Lord Thanet replied. "What does a chit like you know of what is good for this country? The people have been turned from the true faith, they have been blinded by this glittering, gaudy female who has refused to take unto herself a husband, even though His Majesty of Spain proffered her his hand.'

'And rightly so,' Andora replied. 'Would you have England lying under the heel of another country? You are a traitor, my Lord! A traitor to this country and to all Englishmen who are prepared to die for freedom.'

'I have no time to bandy words with you,' Lord Thanet said roughly. 'What I have come to find out is will you or will you not marry my son?'

'I will not,' Andora said.

He opened the door wider and beckoned to someone who was outside. Three men came into the room — the man who had been there when she arrived and whom she now knew to be a priest, and two other men who Andora guessed by their rough and weatherbeaten complexions were messengers. The type of men who travelled through all sorts and conditions of weather, by ship or by road, intent on one thing only — to arrive with all possible speed at their destination.

'She has refused,' Lord Thanet said to the priest.

'Then she must talk,' he answered.

He walked towards Andora, towering above her, making her feel small and insignificant as he said in his deep voice:

'Do you know what we require of you?'

'That I should marry Lord Murton,' she replied.

'No, that you have already refused,' he said. 'We want you to tell us what was said in the Queen's chamber about Francis Drake and the fleet under his command.'

Andora drew in her breath.

'If you refer to the day when I was left behind by the Maids-of-Honour in Her Majesty's chamber then I must tell you that I fell asleep.'

'And you heard nothing?'

'Nothing of any consequence.'

'That is for us to judge,' the priest said. 'Tell me exactly what was said.'

His eyes were looking down into Andora's. She felt almost as if he was trying to mesmerise her in into telling him what he wished to know.

'I cannot remember,' Andora said.

'I think you remember very well,' he said slowly. 'When you awoke the Admiral was there?'

'What Admiral?' Andora asked. 'I am new at Court. I do not recognise people easily.'

'What was he saying?' the priest enquired. 'Did he tell the Queen the latest news of Drake's movements?'

'How do I know what would be the latest news?' Andora asked.

'He spoke then of Drake?'

'Did he? As I have told you, I was asleep.'

Lord Thanet interrupted.

'When you first awoke, you must have heard them speaking,' he said. 'What were they saying?'

'I do not know.'

'I think you lie,' he shouted.

He reached out his hand suddenly and slapped her hard across the face. Andora gave a little cry of shock and surprise.

Lord Murton turned away and walked towards the window.

No one else in the room moved.

'Y. . . you hit me!' Andora said.

It was more an exclamation of astonishment than an accusation.

'I shall hit you again and it will go worse still with you if you do not answer my question,' Lord Thanet replied. 'What did the Admiral tell the Queen?'

Andora felt her anger burn within her. She had been prepared to prevaricate, to pretend she knew nothing. But the blow, instead of intimidating her, had merely made her angry.

'I should think you have realised by now,' she said, looking Lord Thanet straight in the eyes, 'that I am no traitor and I am not prepared to betray Her Majesty or any of her subjects to the friends of Spain.'

'We will soon test your resolution,' he replied. 'Let me give you one more chance. Tell what you know and then you will be allowed to marry my son, if he still desires you.'

'I see now that you believe a wife will not

268

testify against her husband,' Andora answered. 'That is why both he and you are pressing me into marriage. Well, I assure you that, now I see him for what he is, if I were married to him fifty times over I would do everything in my power to bring him to justice.'

'You little fool!' Lord Thanet thundered. 'Can you not realise that you will die for what you have said?'

'I am not afraid,' Andora answered. 'And I would not wish to live if I had to bear the name of a man which would stink in the nostrils of all decent and loyal people.'

She drew a deep breath and went on:

'I will not tell you what you want to know. I am prepared to die with my secret still within me and my answer to all your questions is the same: "God save the Queen!"'

She saw the expression of fury darken Lord Thanet's whole face. He turned abruptly on his heel towards the priest.

'You have heard what she says?' he asked. 'We will make her tell us. Bring my whip. When she tastes pain she will soon change her mind.'

Lord Murton moved swiftly towards his father.

'Father, I beg of you, do not do this,' he pleaded. 'I have seen this happen before. I cannot bear that this should happen to the woman I love.'

'You failed to make her speak,' his father said roughly. 'And you have heard what she said about you. Do you wish to marry her under such circumstances?'

'She does not know what she is saying,' Lord Murton said.

'But I do,' Andora interposed, 'and I beg you not to plead for me. I assure you that is a humiliation that is greater than anything else — that you, in your treachery, should ask mercy for me.'

'You have heard her,' Lord Thanet said roughly. 'If you are too squeamish to hear her screams and to bear the sight of her blood, leave us alone. Go and see if the boat is ready to carry the messenger to the ship. The wind is with them and the sooner this information reaches the King the better.'

As he spoke, he was rolling up the sleeves of his doublet, tucking away the lace ruffs which had hung over his hands. And now, at a word from him, one of the messengers fetched from a corner of the room a long whip with a leather thong. He seemed to be testing it with his fingers as he carried it towards Lord Thanet and stood for a moment waiting while he finished freeing his forearms.

Andora watched, fascinated. Somehow she felt this was all unreal and could not, in fact, be happening to her. Only a few hours ago she had been crying because her love for Sir Hengist was unrequited. Now she was in dire peril, for she knew without any doubt that their threats were not idle.

Lord Thanet nodded to the priest who walked across towards Andora and drew her cape from her shoulders.

'You have not changed your mind, my child?' he asked almost gently. 'There is still time. A last minute repentance will be acceptable to us all.'

'For what should I repent?' Andora asked. 'For wanting England to be victorious? As she will be. Have you not heard that next year is to be a year of marvels, when the Queen will reign triumphant over all her enemies?'

She saw the priest's face darken and then suddenly, before she was really expecting it, Lord Thanet thrust him on one side and flung her face downwards over the chair on which she had recently been seated. She felt his hands pull at the neck of her gown, heard the ruff tear, the hooks burst from the eyes, the soft satin split as he dragged it from her shoulders.

Then there was a whistle as the leather

thonged whip whizzed through the air and a searing pain such as she had never experienced in the whole of her life seemed to Andora almost to cut her body in two.

'Dear God, help me to bear this,' she prayed, stifling the screams that rose in her throat and tensing herself for the next blow and the next.

She felt then as if the pain and the agony of it must kill her and yet she went on praying.

'God help me to keep silent. God, do not let me weaken.'

'What did they say? Will you tell us what they said?'

She heard Lord Thanet's questions breaking through her prayers, his voice, loud though it was, seemed to come from far off, to reach her through a barrier of pain and stinging anguish.

With an almost superhuman effort she forced herself to answer him.

'I should ask the Queen,' she said tauntingly. 'Her Majesty would be able to give you more information than I.'

She heard his snort of disgust and then the whip cut through the air once more and involuntarily, because the pain was unbearable, Andora screamed.

'That is better,' she heard one of the other men say. 'A few more, my Lord, and we shall hear the truth.'

'Hengist, I love you,' Andora whispered to herself. 'I love you. I love you.'

In some strange way his name and her profession of love for him strengthened her. She did not scream again, but the pain grew to an agony which made her feel as if her whole body was falling apart and was already in pieces.

'I love you and you will never know it,' whispered her heart. And then, as the lash seared across her once more and she felt the blood spurt beneath it, a merciful darkness swallowed her up and she sank into it gratefully, still murmuring through lips she had bitten in her agony:

'I love you! I love you!'

11

Hengist Wake was worried. He tried to think of other things, but all the time he found himself remembering a white, frightened face and dark shadows under wide eyes which seemed to hold a hint of tears.

'I meant to apologise to her,' he told himself not once but a dozen times.

He could hardly credit it, but he felt that, in fact, he must be responsible for Andora's agitation and look of unhappiness. Why had he been such a fool, he asked himself, as to lose his temper and kiss her so brutally?

This morning in the garden he had meant to explain everything, to offer her his apologies, to say that he had found it difficult to keep up the Court pretence of courtesy and unemotionalism in whatever situation had to be faced.

He had a feeling that she would understand. Her father was a soldier and he must have told her of the blunt manners of men who were used to deeds rather than words.

He found himself fidgeting all the afternoon when he was in attendance on Lord Essex. They played games, they discussed politics, they sat down to cards, but Sir Hengist's mind was wandering until Lord Essex said accusingly:

'What is the matter with you, Hengist? Your body is here, but your mind is far away from us.'

Sir Hengist rose to his feet and threw the cards down on the table.

'That is true enough,' he said, 'and I will ask you to excuse me. I have matters to which I must attend.'

As he walked from the room he heard someone say with a snigger:

'Wake has a lovelorn look. Do not tell me he has been wounded by Master Cupid.'

There was a roar of laughter, but by this time Sir Hengist had shut the door behind him and was walking briskly to another part of the Palace.

He climbed the stairs to the Queen's apartments and was just about to knock at the sitting-room where he knew the Maids-of-Honour congregated, when the door opened and to his astonishment Lilian Malvern came out.

She was looking as beautiful and fresh as if nothing had occurred the night before to make her scream hysterically and swoon not once but half-a-dozen times in his arms. She was wearing a new gown of peacock blue satin embroidered with pearls and she carried a fan of peacock's feathers which seemed to Sir Hengist, for some unaccountable reason as he was not superstitious, an omen of ill fortune.

'Hengist! What a surprise!' she said. 'What can bring you to this part of the Palace?' Her eyes narrowed suspiciously as she spoke.

Sir Hengist bowed.

'I am glad to see you in good health, Lilian.'

'What is past is past,' she said lightly. 'If regrets could bring back the dead, I would spend the day regretting. As it is, I have other things to think about.'

He had often voiced the same sentiments himself, but now her lightness jarred upon him.

'I am glad for your sake that your memory is so short.'

She pouted her mouth at him.

'How pompous you sound today. You might be an old man instead of a young one. What can we do to bring the red blood back into your veins, dear Hengist? It was one of your most attractive assets that you appeared so virile and manly amongst the pale-faced gentlemen who never leave the Banqueting Hall.'

Sir Hengist bowed, but he said nothing. Lilian Malvern smiled up at him.

'Come, I will not tease you further,' she said. 'Let us be friends, for you know how much your friendship means to me. Will you dine with me tonight — alone?'

Her voice lingered on the last word. Sir Hengist was not a squeamish man, but he felt suddenly that he would never again smell the fragrance of tuberoses and lilies without recalling that inanimate figure hanging limply from the carved canopy of a four-poster bed.

'I regret I am already engaged,' he said suavely.

'Then what about tomorrow night?' Lilian Malvern pressed.

'May I let you know later in the day?' he asked. 'I am not sure what arrangements Lord Essex has made.'

'Do not trouble,' she interrupted sharply. 'It is obvious, Hengist, that you do not wish to come.'

She paused as if waiting for him to speak and contradict her. When he said nothing, she touched his arm with her feather fan.

'I must not stand in your way any longer,' she said. 'But I fear, if you are seeking a certain young lady, you are in for a sad disappointment. She has preferred another, Hengist. You will find it difficult to believe, but she has.'

She walked away from him as she spoke, giving him from her dark, expressive eyes a spiteful glance which somehow made him uneasy. He stood looking after her for a moment with a frown on his face, and then knocking on the sitting-room door, he entered without waiting for a reply.

The room was deserted save for Mistress Parry seated in the corner with her cards. She looked up at his entrance, peering at him for a moment short-sightedly. Then when she recognised him she looked surprised.

'Sir Hengist Wake!' she exclaimed rising with difficulty to her feet. 'What brings you here?'

'I am looking for Andora Bland,' Sir Hengist said bluntly.

'I was about to look for her myself,' Mistress Parry replied, 'for my Lady Malvern has just related to me the most perturbing things.'

'What has she told you?' Sir Hengist asked abruptly.

'I cannot credit it. I cannot, really,' Mistress Parry said. 'Such a nice, quiet girl. I would not have expected her to behave like that.'

'Behave like what?' Sir Hengist asked. 'What has Lady Malvern said? If it is anything bad about Andora, I assure you it is in all probability a lie. I know Lilian Malvern. She is not to be trusted.'

'Not trust my Lady Malvern!' Mistress Parry said in surprise. 'Why? I have no reason to disbelieve anything she should tell me. She is a sweet woman, so beautiful and always with a kind word for an old body like myself.'

'Kind because she thinks you have the Queen's ear,' Sir Hengist muttered. 'But let us not talk of her. Tell me what she said about Andora.'

Mistress Parry sank down in the chair she had just vacated.

'I cannot believe it,' she said. 'The Queen will be very angry. Do you remember when Lady Mary Grey ran away? No, you were too young. It was a long time ago. But the Queen was furious. Of course, Sergeant Porter Keyes was not the right suitor for her, but he paid for his presumption in the Fleet Prison and poor little Lady Mary cried alone in the Chiltern Hills.'

Sir Hengist kept his impatience within bounds with the greatest difficulty.

'Never mind about Lady Mary,' he said, his voice sharp and a little irritated. 'That is old history. We are talking about Andora — Andora Bland. What has happened to her?'

Mistress Parry sighed.

'That naughty child. Why could she not have come to me and asked my advice?'

'What has she done?' Sir Hengist asked. 'Tell me, in God's name! What has she done?'

Mistress Parry glanced over her shoulder as if she thought the very walls were listening.

'Lady Malvern says she has run away to be married.'

'I do not believe it!'

Sir Hengist's voice, loud and aggressive, seemed to echo round the room.

'I do not believe it,' he repeated, bringing his fist down on the card table with such force that the cards jumped and Mistress Parry's hands flew to her breast.

'That is what my Lady Malvern said,' she quavered.

'I do not care what Lady Malvern or any of her ilk say,' Sir Hengist retorted. 'I do not believe it of Andora. When did she go? And with whom?'

'My Lady Malvern did not know that,' Mistress Parry replied. 'But I do not think we shall have to look far to find the man who loves her. Why, he was here this very morning, talking about her and revealing his heart in every word he uttered.'

'Are you referring to Lord Murton?' Sir Hengist asked.

'Who else?' Mistress Parry replied. 'If ever a man wore his heart for all to see, it is he.'

'Do you believe that Andora has run away with him?' Sir Hengist asked. 'It is a lie! She would do no such thing. If she is missing, then she is somewhere in the Palace. I will find her and then I will have such falsehoods stopped at the source from which they are coming.'

He seemed to be talking more to himself than to Mistress Parry who was paying little attention to him.

'A nice young man, Lord Murton,' she was saying in her soft, hesitant voice. 'He spoke of Andora so sweetly. "Tell me about her, Mistress Parry," he said. And I told him how kind she was, how gentle and obedient.'

'Obedient is the right word,' Sir Hengist agreed. 'Andora would never flaunt the Queen's wishes and go off in such a manner without permission, without letting anyone know what were her intentions.'

'The Queen will be very angry,' Mistress Parry said. 'I do not wish to be the one to tell her. "My little country mouse", that is what Her Majesty called Andora; and, as I was telling Lord Murton, there were not many Maids-of-Honour whom she would treat with such kindness and gentleness as Andora.'

'It is no use talking here,' Sir Hengist said almost roughly. 'We must look for her. Where is she likely to be?'

He walked across the room as he spoke to look out of the window, his eyes searching the green lawns sloping down to the river. Surely Andora must be there or in the gardens at the back of the Palace.

'I have never known the Queen so soft-hearted with anyone,' Mistress Parry was saying. 'As I told Lord Murton, any other Maid-of-Honour would have been severely punished for remaining behind when the Queen was in secret audience with an Admiral of the Fleet. But when I apologised for Andora, the Queen said it was no matter; she could trust her country mouse.'

As if her quavering voice suddenly reached Sir Hengist's consciousness, he turned from the window abruptly, his whole body alight as he moved swiftly across the room to Mistress Parry's side.

'What was that you said?' he asked. 'Did you speak of a secret audience? And Andora was present?'

'I was just saying how unexpectedly gentle the Queen was with Andora,' Mistress Parry replied. 'It showed her affection for the girl. As I said to Andora at the time, anyone else would have been severely punished.'

'What did you say she did?' Sir Hengist asked.

'I have just been telling you,' Mistress Parry replied. 'We were told to withdraw from the Queen's apartment because Her Majesty was to give a private audience to one of the Admirals of the Fleet. We all knew, of course, that he would have news of Sir Francis Drake and we moved reluctantly from the chamber, hoping to have a glimpse of him.'

She smiled in remembrance before she went on:

'A fine, upstanding man he was, but when we were all in the ante-room we sat sewing and talking and I must admit that I forgot that Andora should have been with us.'

'She was left behind?' Sir Hengist asked.

'Yes, the stupid child had fallen asleep. When she awoke, she appeared from behind a piece of furniture; but instead of being angry Her Majesty merely laughed.'

Mistress Parry paused to let her words sink in and then she went on:

'It was I who reprimanded Andora — and I must admit that she apologised very prettily.'

'News of Drake!' Sir Hengist said almost to himself. 'Now remember, Mistress Parry, to whom have you told this story? Think now. Who else has heard that Andora was present on this occasion?'

'No one, no one at all,' Mistress Parry answered, 'save Lord Murton and yourself.'

'Lord Murton! You told him this?'

'Yes, indeed, but only because we were talking of Andora.'

'You old fool!'

Sir Hengist said the words so quietly that for a moment Mistress Parry did not take in the full insult of them. Then she looked up into his face and she was no longer angry but apologetic.

'You mean . . . that I should not have spoken of such things?' she said. 'But . . . but only to Lord Murton. He loves Andora and will speak of it to no one.'

'It is enough that he should know,' Sir Hengist said grimly.

'You mean I have . . . done wrong?' Mistress Parry quavered.

'Wrong!' Sir Hengist ejaculated. 'You may have signed Andora's death warrant!'

He flung himself from the room slamming the door behind him. In the passage outside he saw a maidservant.

'Which is Mistress Bland's bedchamber?' he asked.

She looked at him in a startled manner and pointed to a door a short way down the corridor. He walked up to it, rapped with his knuckles and then lifted the latch.

The room was empty. He glanced around him as if searching for something — something to guide or assist him. He saw the unfinished letter on the writing-desk. He picked it up and began to read what Andora had written in her small, delicate handwriting.

He saw it was to her father. At first she spoke of the banquet the Queen had given the night before; the arrival of the various Ambassadors; of her friendship with Lady Mary Howard. Then, after various blots and crossings out, as if she had begun and then changed her mind, then changed it again, she had written:

I do not know how to tell you this, but my heart is no longer in my own keeping. I love . . .

The letter broke off there and Sir Hengist stood staring at it for a long time. For the first time he began to doubt his own intuition, to believe that Lilian Malvern was right and Andora had, indeed, eloped.

The door opened behind him and he turned smartly, the letter still in his hand. Grace came into the room and dropped a curtsy.

'You are Mistress Bland's maid?' Sir Hengist asked.

'I am, Sir.'

'Have you any idea where she is? Have you seen her?'

'No, Sir.'

'There is a rumour in the Palace,' Sir Hengist said, 'that she has run away to be married. Do you think that is possible?'

'Run away!' Grace said in astonishment. 'I am sure, Sir, it is the greatest falsehood. Mistress Andora would never do such a thing. Besides, there is no one she cares for in that way.'

'How do you know?' Sir Hengist enquired harshly.

'I have talked with her, Sir. And I know that although she has been unhappy lately, it is not for love of the gentleman who sends her flowers and notes every day.'

'And who might that be?' Sir Hengist asked.

Grace pursed her lips together as if she felt she should not speak.

'Listen, girl,' Sir Hengist said, 'your mistress may be in danger. Do you understand? In grave danger. But they say that she has run away to be married and we must first ascertain if this story is true.'

'I am sure, Sir, it is one of the many lies that are circulating in this evil place,' Grace answered.

'Then where is she?' Sir Hengist asked, 'if you do not think she has married Lord Murton?'

Grace tossed her head.

'Indeed, Sir, Mistress Andora would have none of him. I have seen her face when his flowers have been brought to her; and the other day she flung them on the floor, crushing the blossoms, and when I would have picked them up she commanded me to throw them away.'

'And if she is not with Lord Murton, where is she?' Sir Hengist asked.

Grace glanced round the room into the cupboard.

'She will not have gone to be married, Sir, of that I am sure,' she said. 'Look! All that Mistress Andora has taken is her warm cloak. Everything else is in its place.'

'Why should she have taken that?' Sir Hengist mused, 'unless Lady Malvern is right?'

Grace moved swiftly to his side.

'Lady Malvern!' she interrupted.

'Yes,' Sir Hengist replied. 'It was Lady Malvern who told Mistress Parry that your mistress had eloped.'

'I will find out the truth of this,' Grace said. 'Wait here, Sir, if it pleases you. I will not be more than a few moments.'

She ran from the room leaving Sir Hengist to pace restlessly up and down. Once he stopped to put out his hand to touch the white pillow where Andora had laid her head. Another time he went to the open door of the cupboard and stood looking at her gowns. They were so small they might have been in the wardrobe of a child. And yet he knew that Andora was in every way a woman.

The door burst open and Grace came hurrying into the room, bringing another maid with her.

'This is Alice, if it please you, Sir,' she said breathlessly to Sir Hengist. 'She is Milady Malvern's maid and is prepared to speak the truth because we are old friends.'

'Do you know anything of this story that

Mistress Bland has run away?' Sir Hengist asked.

Alice curtsied a little nervously.

'Yes, Sir. Her Ladyship made me come here to tell Mistress Bland that Ned Fowler, a boy from her village, had escaped from prison and was waiting to see her in a carriage outside the gates.'

'And was he?' Sir Hengist asked.

'I do not know, Sir. I only said what Lady Malvern told me to say.'

'How did Lady Malvern know the man's name?'

'I think Lord Murton told her about him, Sir.'

'How was that?' Sir Hengist enquired.

'Walter, that is her Ladyship's footman, goes to a tavern near the Palace; and he said that this morning when he called for a glass of ale some time before noon, one of Lord Murton's men was there and asking everyone if they came from Buntingford in Hertfordshire.'

'And did he find anyone from those parts?' Sir Hengist enquired.

'Yes, indeed, Sir. There was a carrier who had come through this very day.'

'And what did the man learn from him?'

'Walter did not know, but he heard them talking and overheard the name of Mistress

Bland and something about being kind to a man called Ned Fowler. He told me this after Lord Murton had been to see her Ladyship early in the afternoon.'

'Do you know what happened when he called?' Sir Hengist asked.

'No, Sir, for I was not in the room. But as his Lordship opened the door to leave I heard her Ladyship say: ". . . Ned Fowler, and he is in prison." And his Lordship said: "I cannot thank you enough but I shall try the other way first. I will tell my page to say there is someone from her home at the gates. It is always a mistake to mention people unless one is absolutely certain they are alive." '

'His Lordship left then,' Alice went on. 'But when I went into the drawing-room, her Ladyship had a purse of gold in her hands. She held it up to the light. "Look at that, Alice," she said to me. "That will be useful and if you are a good girl you shall have some of the wages that I owe you." '

'A little later his Lordship's page called with a note. I do not know what was in it, but immediately after her Ladyship had read it, she made me go with her to Mistress Bland's room and told me what I must say about Ned Fowler.'

Sir Hengist had listened to Alice's story

without moving and without taking his eyes
from her face. Now he drew a gold piece
from the purse at his waist and put it into
her hand.

'Thank you, Alice,' he said. 'You have
helped me more than I believed possible.
Tell me one thing more. Are you certain
that Lord Murton did not say where he was
going?'

'No, Sir.'

Sir Hengist put his hand on Grace's
shoulder.

'What you have done in bringing this girl
to me may save your mistress's life,' he said.
'But speak of this to no one. Do you understand? No one in the Palace. And both of
you go down on your knees, for she needs
your prayers.'

He went from the room leaving them
gaping after him; and hurrying down the
long corridors to the other side of the
Palace, he came to Lord Murton's apartments. He hammered on the door and after
some minutes it was opened by a page with
his coat unbuttoned and his hair tousled as
if he had just awoken from a sleep.

'Where is your master?' Sir Hengist enquired.

'He has gone away, Sir.'

'Where to?'

'I do not know, Sir. He did not say.'

'Are you quite sure of that?' Sir Hengist questioned.

'Quite sure, Sir. He did not tell me where he was going.'

'When did he leave?'

'About two hours ago, Sir.'

'In a carriage?'

'Oh, no, Sir, on horseback.'

'Are you quite certain of that?'

'Quite certain, Sir. He asked for his riding clothes; and when his valet had dressed him, a message came from the stables that his horse was ready for him.'

'Who else is here?' Sir Hengist asked.

'No one, Sir. They have all gone out. They always do when the master is away.'

Sir Hengist drew a gold piece from his purse.

'Do you see this?' he said. 'If you can tell me where your master has gone or if you can give me even a hint of his destination, it shall be yours.'

The page's eyes glinted greedily, but he shook his head with obvious reluctance.

'He did not tell me anything, Sir,' he said and there was no doubt at all that the boy was speaking in all sincerity.

Sir Hengist made to put the coin back in his purse and then, seeing the look of disappointment on the boy's face, he threw the coin in the air.

'I suppose you have done your best,' he muttered and went back towards the Queen's apartments the way he had come.

Entering them, he strode past the Maids-of-Honours' rooms and into the ante-room, where he found Lady Mary Howard and four of the other ladies.

'Good evening, Sir Hengist!' Lady Mary said, a smile lighting her sweet face.

'Where is Her Majesty?' Sir Hengist asked abruptly.

'Engaged with a visitor,' Lady Mary answered. 'And being so long in conference with him that we feel we shall all be late for dinner. One hour he has been here now and not a sign of his departure.'

'Who is with the Queen?' Sir Hengist asked.

'Who but the famous Doctor Dee!' Lady Mary replied.

'By all that is Holy!' Sir Hengist exclaimed. 'He is the very man I need. If he is a real magician, we shall know the truth once and for all.'

He walked towards the inner door. Lady Mary gave an exclamation and rose as if to stop him.

'You cannot interrupt Her Majesty, Sir Hengist.'

'I have every intention of doing just that,' Sir Hengist answered, and went into the inner room without stopping to knock.

The Queen was sitting at a small table in the window facing Doctor Dee, the astrologer and magician. When Elizabeth first ascended the throne, Mistress Blanche Parry had introduced Doctor Dee who had consulted the stars in order to fix an auspicious day for the coronation.

Since then he had come constantly to Court at Elizabeth's invitation and she had even visited his house at Mortlake. There he had shown her his magic mirror in which girls could expect to see the features of their future husbands, and the great crystal in which the Doctor would read both the future and the past lives of his clients.

He was a tall, thin man wearing a long black robe. A skull cap covered his bald head and he had a long, white beard flowing down his chest. As Sir Hengist entered, he was muttering strange incantations to himself as he peered into the crystal which lay between him and the Queen on a square of black velvet.

Elizabeth looked up sharply.

'What do you want, Sir Hengist?' she asked. 'Can you not see that I am busy?'

'My business, Your Majesty, is not with

you,' Sir Hengist replied, 'but with Doctor Dee. I have most urgent need of his services.'

'Indeed!' the Queen exclaimed. 'And what do you consider more important than that his Queen should consult him on matters of importance to the State?'

Sir Hengist went down on one knee.

'Your Majesty! One of your Maids-of-Honour is in dire peril. She has been spirited away from here and there is a rumour that she has eloped in order to get married.'

The Queen's face darkened.

'One of my Maids-of-Honour married without my permission!' she ejaculated, and her voice rose on the last word.

'I do not believe it to be the truth, Your Majesty,' Sir Hengist said. 'I think there are other reasons why she has been compelled to leave the Palace.'

He accentuated the word 'compelled' and the Queen's eyes met his.

'Who is it?' she asked.

'Mistress Andora Bland,' Sir Hengist replied.

He saw the anger fade from the Queen's face and knew she understood.

'You mean she has vanished?' she asked in a low voice.

'I know who has taken her, Your Majesty; but I do not know where they have gone. I believe that it is a question of time as to whether she can be saved.'

The Queen turned imperiously towards the old man listening to them.

'Doctor Dee,' she said. 'You have heard what we have said. Andora Bland is one of my Maids-of-Honour. Look into your crystal and see where she is at this moment. Look carefully, for her life may depend on your seeing the exact place where Sir Hengist must go if he is to prevent a tragedy from taking place.'

It was like the Queen, Sir Hengist thought, that she should grasp so quickly all that he had implied in but a few words, and he reflected that when there was real danger or action to be taken, she never failed either those who served her or the country.

He rose to his feet.

'I have never believed in the occult before,' he said, 'but if you can tell me now where I should look for Mistress Bland, I will never doubt your powers again.'

'I need something which belongs to her,' Doctor Dee said.

'I will send post-haste to her chamber ...' the Queen began, only to be silenced as Sir Hengist drew from his doublet a small, lace-edged handkerchief.

'Mistress Bland dropped it in the garden,'

he said shamefacedly by way of explanation.

He did not see the little smile of amusement on the Queen's lips or the glint of understanding in her shrewd eyes.

Doctor Dee cradled the crystal in the handkerchief. Then he stared into it for what seemed to Sir Hengist a long time.

'I can see a girl who is frightened,' he said at length. 'There is blood in the crystal and the shadow of treachery.'

'Yes, yes, we know all that,' Sir Hengist said quickly. 'Where do you see her? That is what matters.'

'It is not a place I have ever seen before,' Doctor Dee replied. 'It is a castle and there is water near it.'

'It might apply to a hundred places in the kingdom,' Sir Hengist exclaimed in exasperation.

'It is a castle,' Doctor Dee repeated, 'but I see wings around it — the wings of birds flying.'

He took no notice of Sir Hengist's snort of impatience.

'Birds flying . . . many birds. They are . . . Yes, they are ducks.'

'Ducks!' Sir Hengist murmured, and then with a sudden shout which seemed almost to rock the pictures on the walls he cried: 'God's truth! 'Tis the Castle Mallard! I have not thought of it for many years. A perfect hiding place and near enough to the Earl of Thanet's own estates. Yet on the river — the river, Your Majesty, up which the ships come and go from foreign lands.'

'Castle Mallard!' the Queen said. 'I have heard of it, but I have never been there.'

'It was repaired by Your Majesty's father for the duck shooting,' Sir Hengist told her. 'And that is why he christened it with the name of the ducks he brought down so skilfully with his bow.'

Sir Hengist dropped again on to one knee.

'Have I Your Majesty's leave to go there at once to find Andora Bland?' he said.

Elizabeth rose to her feet.

'Go, Sir Hengist, with all possible despatch,' she said. 'Take any of my gentlemen or horses that you deem necessary. And God go with you.'

He kissed her hand and was gone from the room almost before she had finished speaking. He ran through the ante-chamber, leaving the Maids-of-Honour staring after him in surprise. He sped down the corridors and through the Long Gallery until he came to the card room where a number of gentlemen were engaged in passing the time and losing large sums of money to each other.

He stood for a moment in the doorway taking stock of who was present. To his relief he saw three of his closest friends.

'Sherborne! Derby! Percival!' he called them. 'To horse on the Queen's business!'

They did not stop to ask questions. They knew by Sir Hengist's face that something urgent was afoot and within ten minutes they were clattering out of the Palace yard, their horses rearing and prancing, their cloaks flying out behind them in the wind.

'To Castle Mallard!' Sir Hengist said aloud, and added beneath his breath: 'And God help little Andora if we are not in time.'

12

There was darkness and pain shooting through it in crimson waves. There was a long, dark tunnel which she was forced to traverse whether she wished it or no. And then suddenly in the midst of the darkness there came a voice, high and hysterical, shouting so that it seemed as if the sound of it must deafen her.

'You have killed her! You have killed her! What good will she be to us if she be dead?'

'She is not dead,' another voice said, deep yet hard. 'She is but unconscious. His Lordship struck too hard.'

'I forgot she was a woman and frail. I thought of her only as an enemy of the true Church, a heretic who should be punished for opposing us.'

'If she dies, you will learn nothing.'

Andora could hear the bitterness and a note almost of despair in Lord Murton's voice.

Now she remembered where she was. Now the horror of what had happened to her came flooding over her and the pain at her back mingled with the feeling of humiliation because they had forced her to scream.

She did not open her eyes. She lay hoping they would still think her unconscious.

'You should have let me try my methods, my Lord,' she heard the priest say.

'Very well,' Lord Thanet said in irritated tones. 'Have it your own way. I will do no more. But why should we be held up because some chit of a girl defies us? You cannot force the truth out of her, Father, save by the whip.'

'Women need more subtle methods,' the priest replied. 'In Spain we have much evidence that at the time of the Inquisition direct violence incited them merely to be martyrs.'

'Then what do you suggest?' Lord Thanet asked.

'First we will awaken her,' the priest answered.

Andora was tense, wondering what they would do and yet praying that her air of unconsciousness might persuade them to be lenient. What she did not expect was a shower of icy cold water straight in her face.

She started, gasped, opened her eyes and raised herself to wipe the water away with

301

hands that felt weak and ineffective.

'She is alive!' Lord Murton said in relief.

'Yes, she is alive,' Lord Thanet answered, 'and much good may it do her. Now, Father, what is your key to unlock this secret that she holds between her lips?'

'I will tell you what it is,' the priest said slowly and deliberately, and Andora knew that he was speaking to her rather than to Lord Thanet. 'We have found that the most exquisite and, indeed, unbearable pain can be involved by the use of slivers of wood hammered underneath the fingernails.'

Involuntarily and without her conscious volition Andora heard her own voice crying:

'No! No!'

'You see,' the priest said, 'already she is afraid. Already she knows that sooner or later the pain which we shall invoke will make her speak.'

He bent down towards her, his face almost level with hers.

'Why not speak now?' he asked.

Andora shut her eyes so that she should not see his face, his dark, mesmeric eyes staring into hers. She pressed her lips tightly together too, determined that she would say nothing. It was all too easy to start talking and not to know where to stop.

The priest straightened himself.

'Start preparing the wood,' he said to the two messengers standing behind them. 'It must be hard and must be capable of being whittled by your knives into a fine point — the finer the better. It enters first like a needle and then gradually grows broader, splitting the nail from the hand with every blow of the hammer.'

'Stop!' Lord Murton cried. 'Wait one moment while I talk to Andora. Let me speak with her alone. Let me persuade her to tell us what we want to know before she suffers in such a manner.'

'There is no time,' his father answered angrily, only to be silenced by the raised hand of the priest.

'There is time while we prepare the wooden nails,' he said. 'I suggest, Your Lordship, that we withdraw to the far end of the room. While we are working we shall not overhear what is said and if your son can persuade this woman to see sense it will save us time and her unnecessary pain.'

'Very well, I agree,' Lord Thanet said ungraciously. 'But you had best hurry, my son, for the tide will not wait for women or the false pride of heretics who should be burned at the stake.'

He turned as he spoke and walked to the far end of the room followed by the priest

303

and the other men who were already drawing out their knives and seeking a likely piece of wood amongst the furniture in the room.

Lord Murton dropped on his knees beside Andora's chair.

'Listen, Andora,' he said. 'You have been brave long enough. Listen to me, for your obstinacy will avail you nothing. Can you not understand that now you will die anyway, whether you tell them what they want to know or whether you keep silent?'

His eyes rested on her white, frightened face and fair hair curling beneath the water which had wetted it.

'You are too young, too pretty to die,' he said and his voice was soft and caressing. 'But if death must come to you, let it come peacefully and not in screaming agony with your fingers deformed and your body twisted in pain.'

'I will . . . tell them nothing,' Andora answered, trying to speak defiantly but aware with a sudden horror that the voice coming between her lips did not sound like her own, it was so weak and hoarse.

'You think you are being a martyr and you think that you will save England by your defiance,' Lord Murton said sadly. 'But, Andora, I will tell you something. The sacrifice of yourself is quite unnecessary. We know other things besides what you can tell us.'

'How do you imagine you can explain away my death?' Andora asked.

'There will be no explaining,' he answered, 'for I am not returning to the Palace. We are all leaving tonight for Spain, for my mission at the Court is finished.'

'Her Majesty is well rid of you,' Andora whispered.

'She will miss me more than you credit,' Lord Murton said. 'For I can tell you now, Andora, that I take with me Lord Burleigh's book containing details of all the ships in Her Majesty's Navy.'

'How is it possible for you to have that?' Andora asked, wishing to disbelieve him.

'Old men are stupid and too trusting,' Lord Murton replied. 'I was talking with Lord Burleigh in his room — by deliberate connivance, of course — when a messenger came to tell him that the Queen required his presence immediately. He left me alone for only a few moments, but long enough for me to discover the book of Her Majesty's Navy and, what was even more important, a missive on which was written the names of all the British agents in Spain, France and the Low Countries.'

He was boasting, Andora knew, but boasting so convincingly that she could not help but believe him.

'It is not true. You are inventing this,' she said; but her instinct told her that it was, indeed, the truth and her heart sank at the full import of what this would mean to England's enemies.

All the men named in the missive would be put to death, being hanged, drawn and quartered or burned at the stake. It was not so much the loss of such informers that mattered, but the fact that if, indeed, as Lord Murton said, he had the whole list of those engaged in assisting England, then the Queen would be hard put for information which was of vital importance for the defence of the country.

'I have been clever,' Lord Murton bragged. 'Who suspected me? Quiet, charming, good-looking Lord Murton. Who remembered that my father had once quarrelled with Lord Burleigh and left the Court vowing vengeance not only on him but on the woman who had driven our priests into hiding and made all good Catholics afraid to profess the true faith.'

'You are English,' Andora said. 'How can you want us to be conquered by a foreign country? And, above all, by Spain?'

'Did King Philip conquer us when he was married to Mary?' Lord Murton retorted. 'If Elizabeth had accepted the honour of his hand, as she should have done, then the two countries could have dwelt together amicably. Now it is too late. You shall all suffer under the heel of Spain and learn who are your masters.'

'I cannot understand how anyone was deceived by you,' Andora said.

'If there had been time, you would have loved me,' he replied conceitedly.

She shook her head even though it was painful to do so.

'Never!' she answered. 'I never loved you nor was there any chance of my doing so. And when you kissed me I knew that there was something wrong about you although I did not know to what depths you had sunk.'

'I shall remember that kiss,' Lord Murton said reflectively, looking at her lips. 'You are so soft, sweet and feminine, Andora. It is a pity you must be so stupid about this very small matter of telling my father what he wants to know. Had you been sensible, you would have been my wife and I would have taken you with me on the *Rose of Wapping* when she sails tonight for Spain.'

'I would have thrown myself overboard rather than have allowed you to touch me,'

Andora said. 'Your fingers are dripping with the blood of Englishmen. The information you are carrying to Spain may result not only in the death of many who come from the same soil as yourself, it may also result in the sinking of our ships, the destruction of the Queen's Navy.'

'Let us hope it does,' Lord Murton said callously. 'What I am concerned with now is saving you, Andora.'

'But I will not accept your help,' she replied. 'Let me die. It does not matter. Death is preferable to life if one must be a traitor, lower than the basest reptile which crawls upon the face of the earth.'

'Look at your hands,' he said. 'Look at those long, white fingers that you have tended so well, those little rosy nails. Do you know what they will be like when they have finished torturing you? Listen to me, Andora, I have seen men under torture. They tell in the end. The truth bursts from them even though they try with all their heart and soul not to say it. There is always a point at which their will-power breaks, at which their brain gives way. Save yourself from that.'

Andora raised her hands to her ears and shut her eyes.

'I will not listen to you,' she whispered. 'I cannot.'

'You are young, Andora, and you have seen so little of the world. You do not understand that women should not meddle in these things. It is men who must fight for what they believe to be right. A woman's job is to love them and to bear their children, not to argue about matters which do not concern them.'

'There is a woman on the Throne of England,' Andora answered taking her hands from her ears and opening her eyes again. 'Could I betray her and thus assist in the destruction not only of my country but of my sex?'

'The Queen is not a real woman,' Lord Murton replied contemptuously. 'She is but a symbol, an illusion, which Englishmen worship because they have forsaken the true God and the true faith.'

'That is not true,' Andora answered angrily. 'And I will tell you something which when you reach Spain you would do well to remember. Whether you kill me and all the men named on the missive that you have stolen from Lord Burleigh matters little. Whether you sink our ships and capture Sir Francis Drake unawares matters only for the moment. England will remain free — free of all her enemies who, like Spain, seek to destroy her because they are envious both of her courage and her happiness.'

Lord Murton stared at her and then he crossed himself.

'You speak as if you prophesy,' he muttered. 'Sometimes those who are near to death tell truths greater than themselves.'

'I speak of what I know will happen,' Andora said. 'Reptiles like you and your father cannot destroy something that is as great and wonderful as this country of ours. Spain will not be victorious, and next year — the Year of Wonders — perhaps we shall destroy Spain.'

'Andora, you frighten me,' Lord Murton cried. 'Do not let us talk of such things. Time is running out.'

He glanced over his shoulder as he spoke.

'They are nearly ready for you. Andora! Give in! Tell them that you will reveal everything you know now and at once if they will permit you to marry me. Make it a condition. I think they will agree because the tide is turning and we must be away.'

'Why should you want me, a heretic, as your wife?' Andora asked.

'Because I love you,' he said. 'Love, after all, is stronger than hate. I hate England; I hate Elizabeth and all she stands for. But I love you. I want to hold you in my arms, to kiss you, to feel your lips again beneath mine. I love you, Andora. Tell them, as I have said, that you will reveal what was said in the Queen's private audience once you are my wife.'

'I would rather marry a swineherd who is loyal to the Crown,' Andora said quietly, 'or the commonest thief due to be hanged at Tyburn. I think your offer is meant kindly; but cannot you understand that I despise you utterly? The very thought of being near you makes my flesh creep.'

Lord Murton stared despairingly at her as if at last he was bereft of words and could no longer plead his cause.

'We are ready,' Lord Thanet said from the end of the room. 'If you have not persuaded her to speak, my son, then let the good Father try his wiles upon her. They will, I am convinced, prove more persuasive than your tongue.'

'Do you hear that, Andora?' Lord Murton said. 'Quick, this is your last chance. Say what you have to say, I beg and pray of you.'

'I cannot,' Andora replied. 'You know that I cannot. You must go your way and I must go mine. But remember as you sail towards Spain that I have cursed you; cursed you for what you are and all you stand for; cursed you from now until the last breath that you draw.'

She saw that he shivered and then the priest spoke.

'We must hurry,' he said. 'Come, my Lord, if she has not agreed by now then we must try what these little pieces of wood will do — for I swear they are very eloquent.'

'Andora!' Lord Murton cried imploringly. And then as she did not reply he said in a whisper so that those approaching could not hear. 'Let me kiss you good-bye. Let me remember for all time the warmth of those lips which will soon be cold in death. Kiss me and let me believe that if times had been happier and we had not been in opposition we might have found contentment together.'

His face drew nearer to hers. With an effort which made her wince because of the weals upon her back, Andora raised her hand and putting all her failing strength behind the blow, struck him in the face.

'The rack would be preferable to the touch of your lips,' she said. 'Go to Spain and may God heap all the fires of hell upon your black soul!'

He winced away from her, startled by her blow and even more by her words.

As the priest drew Andora from the chair in which she had been sitting, she heard him mutter a prayer and then with all the dignity

312

she could muster, holding her torn dress around her, she walked down the room to where the other men stood waiting.

Two chairs were placed facing each other across a narrow polished table. On it were ten nails of wood, very sharp and pointed at one end, blunt and round at the other.

'One for each finger,' Andora thought, and beside them was a carpenter's wooden hammer.

'You will seat yourself in this chair,' the priest said to Andora indicating a hard, upright, wooden chair with high arms. 'I could bind you,' he said, 'but all this takes time and so my good friends have offered to hold you in your place. They are strong and inclined to be rough, so I advise you not to fight against them unnecessarily.'

Andora moistened her lips with the tip of her tongue, but she said nothing. Already she could feel a tingling at the tips of her fingers where she knew the pain would begin. But it was not pain of which she was afraid but her own weakness.

Now that she had to die, she knew that her father would expect her to die as became his daughter — both with dignity and courage. She tried to think of him lying on his bed at home, having no idea what trials she must undergo. But somehow he seemed vague and far away.

It was Sir Hengist she clung to in her mind, seeing him so strong and debonair, his head thrown back in laughter as if he defied the whole world with his very strength and virility.

'I love you, Hengist!' She whispered his name to herself.

'Hengist! Hengist!'

Yet try as she would, she could not stop herself trembling as she seated herself in the chair and the two men standing beside it pressed it hard against the table. The priest seated himself opposite her.

'Give me your hand,' he said.

She held it out to him and with an almost superhuman effort kept it steady as he took it in his, turning it over first that way and then this as a man might contemplate a piece of wood or stone on which he was about to work.

'Have you any preference as to which nail we shall do first?' he asked, baring his teeth in what was meant to be a smile.

She knew that this was intended to intimidate her and she answered:

'It will be your choice, Sir, whatever preference I profess.'

'Then shall we start with the little finger?' the priest asked. 'I have always believed — though I may be mistaken — that there is more sensitivity in the little finger of a woman's hand than in any other.'

He picked up one of the wooden nails, tested it as if to see how sharp it was, then segregating the small finger of her left hand from the rest, glanced up at the men who stood beside her.

Two heavy hands clamped down on Andora's shoulders, the right hand of the man on her left side held her wrist firmly on the table.

'For the last time,' the priest said, 'will you tell what you know?'

'I shall die with my secret safely locked in my breast,' Andora replied.

'We will see about that,' he said quietly but with such sinister intent in his voice that it was more frightening than if he had ranted and roared at her.

Now the wooden nail was poised only a few centimeters from her finger and he held it as a man will hold a dart, ready to jab it under the nail with a deft movement which would drive it home quite a long way before he reached for the hammer.

Andora held her breath.

'God help me to keep silent,' she prayed. 'God help me to be brave, to show that I am a soldier's daughter.'

The priest struck. She felt the sudden pain shriek up her arm and strike almost like lightning through every nerve in her body. And even as she gritted her teeth together in an effort not to scream out, she heard a voice crying loudly and urgently:

'Andora! Andora!'

The priest glanced over his shoulder. The two men holding her released their grip. She heard Lord Thanet say:

'Quick, my son, through the secret passageway. We will hold them off until you can sail.'

She saw Lord Murton hurl himself across the room towards a bookcase in the corner.

'Andora!'

The call came again and this time she was able to answer.

'I am here! Quick! I am here!'

She saw Lord Murton find the secret spring, the bookcase swung back and behind it was a dark opening in the wall with a flight of steps leading downwards.

The door burst open. The room seemed suddenly full of men and swords flashing one against another in the waning light coming from the window. She saw Sir Hengist drive his sword through the body of the priest, who toppled over as if he were a skittle rather than a human being.

And then Sir Hengist had his arms around her and his voice, unbelievably clear above the tumult, said:

'My darling! My little love! What have they done to you?'

She fought an overwhelming desire to hide her face against his shoulder.

'Lord Murton!' she gasped. 'He has the secrets of the Navy upon him. The secret passage . . .'

'Derby! See to it!' she heard Sir Hengist call over his shoulder, and she saw a man, sword in hand, plunge past the open book-case and down the steps that Lord Murton had taken.

The two men who had held her were both lying on the floor either dead or dangerously wounded. Lord Thanet had been disarmed and now two of Sir Hengist's friends were tying his hands behind his back.

Sir Hengist bent and picked up Andora in his arms, lifting her from the chair. As he did so, he saw her bare back, the blood on her torn gown.

'My God!' he said between his teeth. 'Someone shall pay for this.'

'Lord Murton is going to Spain,' Andora said. 'Stop him! At all cost he must be stopped.'

Sir Hengist, holding her high in his arms,

waited for a moment. Up the stone steps behind the book case came Lord Derby, his sword stained red. Sir Hengist raised his eyebrows.

'Murton?' he asked.

'He is dead,' Lord Derby replied laconically. 'He put up a poor fight. He never was any use as a swordsman.'

'Search his doublet,' Sir Hengist said. 'He has documents on him of some importance.'

Lord Derby turned to obey and Sir Hengist carried Andora out of the room and into the big, empty chamber she had entered first on her arrival at the Castle. There was a wide window-seat with soft cushions on it and here he set her down, doing it as gently as possible, and then, taking from his own shoulders a short, satin-lined cape, he set it on hers to hide her nakedness.

'Andora! Thank God we were in time,' he said in a voice so moved and broken that she looked at him almost in surprise.

He fastened his cape across her white breast and then, lifting her hand in his, kissed the wounded finger from which the blood was flowing.

'They have hurt you,' he said. 'I would make them all die a thousand deaths rather than this should have happened to you.'

The touch of his lips made her realise, as if for the first time, that this was real, it was actually happening. She had prayed for him and he had come. She had wanted him with such intensity that now he was here she felt almost as if it were all a dream.

But he was here and he was speaking to her in a voice that she had never heard before. Now his mouth was against her other fingers, kissing them one by one, until his lips rested in the palm of her hand.

'I thought I was . . . to die,' she said in a wondering voice.

'And yet you did not save yourself by telling them what they wanted to know.'

'How could I?' she said. 'They were sailing for Spain tonight.'

She felt Sir Hengist become suddenly tense.

'Tonight!' he said. 'In what ship?'

'The *Rose of Wapping*. It is waiting in the river for the tide.'

He put down her hand on her lap and sprang to his feet. He walked back towards the room they had just left.

'Sherborne and Percival!' he called. 'Will you ride at once to Tilbury? There will be ships of war in the harbour. Tell them to intercept the *Rose of Wapping* as she sails down the river and take her captain and crew into custody. They would have har-boured these traitors and carried them to Spain.'

'We will go at once,' Lord Percival answered. 'What about the prisoner? He is the only one left alive.'

'More is the pity,' Sir Hengist said with contempt in his voice. 'Take him with you. Put him on my horse. Hand him over to the Military and tell them to convey him to the Tower to await Her Majesty's pleasure.'

'Would you like me to go with them?' Lord Derby enquired. 'The rest of the traitors here are not likely to give you any trouble.'

'No. But we have got to get Andora back to the Palace,' Sir Hengist said. 'And, as you know, there is no roadway for a carriage up to this Castle — which is what makes it so impregnable. Get a boatman. There must be one waiting to carry these swine to the ship. They shall row us back to Greenwich. It will be easier for Andora than travelling on horseback. See about it, Derby, and tell me when you have everything arranged.'

'And then, I suppose, I ride after the others?' Lord Derby asked with a smile.

'That is the idea,' Sir Hengist replied.

The three gentlemen, laughing with delight at what had been accomplished and escorting their silent prisoner, walked past Andora in the great entrance chamber. Then suddenly there was silence. She saw Sir Hengist coming towards her, and as their eyes met she felt as if he drew her heart into his keeping and she was no longer herself but a part of him.

And yet, because she could hardly believe that what he had said when he first came was not part of the delirium of pain, her eyelashes dropped against her cheeks as she waited shyly for him to speak. He seated himself beside her.

'How could you have made me suffer as you did?' he asked.

'Have you suffered?' she enquired.

'If you only knew what I have been through,' he answered, 'knowing you were in danger and not knowing where to find you. God bless the venerable Doctor Dee. I will never laugh at the occult again. If it had not been for him, Andora, you might have been dead by now.'

'They meant to kill me,' she said simply. 'I could have saved myself only by marrying Lord Murton — and that I would rather have died than do.'

'Marry him!' Sir Hengist ejaculated. 'So he offered you that? And I thought you loved him.'

'No, I never loved him,' Andora answered. 'But I was sorry for him because he appeared to love me so greatly.'

'If only I had killed him when I found him kissing you,' Sir Hengist said. 'I could have saved you all this.'

He looked down at her injured finger, checked himself as he would have put his arm around her, and instead laid it very gently behind her on the window-ledge.

'How did you contrive to be so brave?' he asked. 'I expected to hear your screams when we entered the Castle and when there were none I thought they must have killed you already.'

'I screamed once,' Andora said. 'And then . . . then I thought of . . . someone who made me feel brave.'

He waited for her to explain, but when she said no more he told her in a low voice:

'I read the letter to your father that I found in your bedchamber. I hoped it might give me some clue as to where you had gone. In it you spoke of having lost your heart to someone. If it was not Lord Murton, who was it?'

He felt a quiver go through her, not of fear but of a shyness which in itself was almost a delight. And then, looking down at her little face he saw the colour flooding into it.

'Tell me who it is, Andora,' he said, 'for there cannot be any pretence between us at this moment.'

'I . . . I cannot tell you,' Andora stammered, 'for it is . . . someone who I do not . . . think cares for me.'

'Does not care for you!' Sir Hengist said harshly. 'Then in that case it is not the person about whom I thought you might be writing.'

'No?' Andora questioned.

She looked up into his eyes and what she saw there made her draw her breath in sharply.

'I love you, Andora!' Sir Hengist said and his voice was low and deeply moved. 'Did you not know that? Did you not know that I have loved you from the very first moment I saw you peeping out of that broken carriage and heard your little voice scolding me?'

He drew a deep breath.

'I loved you and yet I fought against it because I felt that I had no use for women in my life. It was true until I met you.'

It seemed to Andora as if the hall, in the dusk of the setting sun, was suddenly flooded with a golden light. Instinctively her uninjured hand went out towards Sir Hengist; and now his arm, resting behind her, drew her very gently closer to him.

'I have loved everything about you — your gentleness, your simplicity, your lack of sophistication,' he said. 'The way you seemed so utterly different from all the other women at Court. And yet you drove me mad with jealousy — when I found you in Lord Braye's apartments; when I saw that white-livered boaster, Murton, kissing you by the river-side. Andora, you have much to answer for.'

A smile seemed to light her tired face.

'I . . . I thought you despised me,' she murmured.

He gave a little laugh that was almost a sob.

'My darling, how blind you must have been! Despise you? You who are so brave! Who have proved yourself a soldier's daughter, not only in this but in so many things besides. I am not worthy to kiss the ground on which you walk. And yet, because I love you, because I want you with all my heart and with all my soul, I can only beg of you to marry me.'

Andora felt as if she could not look into his eyes any longer. The wonder and the glory in what she saw there was too much to be borne.

She gave a little cry and hid her face on his shoulder. He kissed her hair and touched her neck with gentle fingers.

'We will be married as soon as you are well enough to travel,' he said. 'I have a house in Devon which is empty and dusty because it needs a mistress. We will go there away from the Court, and the Queen must find another Maid-of-Honour. You have served her valiantly. She cannot ask more of you.'

'I think I have done what they wanted of me,' Andora whispered against his doublet.

He put his fingers under her chin and lifted her face up to his.

'You have done that and so much more besides. Now is the time to think of yourself — and of me.'

'I was thinking of you all the time,' she told him. 'That was what enabled me to endure the pain and kept me from telling the Queen's secret. It was because I thought of you, my . . .'

She hesitated, the blood coming once again to her cheeks. She moved against his fingers, but he would not let her go.

'Say it,' he commanded. 'Let me hear you say it. Your — what?'

'My . . . my love for you,' she whispered.

His lips were on hers. He held her captive, drawing her closer; and though the movement hurt the weals on her back, she did not wince. Instead she gave herself to him wholeheartedly and felt his kiss sweep away everything but the wonder and glory of their love for one another.

This was love! This, she thought, was an adventure far greater than anything she had encountered before this moment.

'I love you, Andora! You are mine! Mine for all time! You belong to me.'

'I love you!' she answered, her lips throbbing against his lips, her heart beating against his.

Lord Derby, opening the door to tell them that the boat was ready, shut it quietly again. There was no hurry, he thought philosophically. Everything — even the report to the Queen of what had happened — must wait for love!

About the Author

Barbara Cartland, who sadly died in May 2000 at the age of nearly ninety-nine, was the world's most famous romantic novelist. She wrote 723 books in her lifetime, with worldwide sales of over one billion copies and her books were translated into thirty-six different languages.

As well as romantic novels, she wrote historical biographies, six autobiographies, theatrical plays, books of advice on life, love, vitamins and cookery. She also found time to be a political speaker and television and radio personality.

She wrote her first book at the age of twenty-one, and this was called Jigsaw. It became an immediate bestseller and sold 100,000 copies in hardback, and was translated into six different languages. She wrote continuously throughout her life, writing bestsellers for an astonishing seventy-six years. Her books have always been immensely popular in the United States, where in 1976 her current books were at numbers one and two in the B. Dalton bestsellers list, a feat never achieved before or since by any author.

Barbara Cartland became a legend in her own lifetime and will be remembered for her wonderful romantic novels, so loved by her millions of readers throughout the world.

Her books will always be treasured for their moral message, her pure and innocent heroines, her good-looking and dashing heroes and above all her belief that the power of love is more important than anything else in everyone's life.